By Way of Autumn
Jacqueline Druga

By Way of Autumn
By Jacqueline Druga
Copyright 2015 by Jacqueline Druga

Thank you so very much to Kira R and to Shona for your editorial help services.

Cover Art by Christian Bentulan
www.coversbychristian.com

ONE – STICKY

July 7

Tell me what to say.

What can I do to make it right?

What's wrong?

Nothing.

But that wasn't the truth. Something was wrong. I just know what it was. How many times over the last year did my husband Jeff ask me what was wrong? "Tess," he would say. "Come on tell me. How can we fix this?"

There was nothing I could tell him. I did have an answer for him but was it one that would really fix it all? I struggled with it myself, trying to find happiness, living day by day, feeling my emotions slip away. I felt horrible because there was absolutely nothing wrong with Jeff. He was a good man, he provided for his family, was there when we needed him. He never cheated or lied.

It was me.

Not that I cheated or lied, I didn't.

There was no question in my mind whether I loved my husband. I did. I just didn't know how much or if it was even the type of love needed to make a marriage work. We were doing something right as we celebrated our seventeenth anniversary on the first of July.

We had a barbeque in the backyard, nothing romantic, no gifts, just a cook out in the backyard because it was too hot to cook in the kitchen.

The air conditioning wasn't working properly and the desert air always seemed to hover and linger over our town a little longer than it should.

We didn't hold hands, kiss, we barely slept in the same bed. It wasn't for lack of trying on Jeff's part.

He was married before me. There is nothing negative to say about Jeff's ex. Samantha was a bright woman, a professor at UCLA. They married young, broke up young, and shared in the raising of their daughter, Nicole.

Without animosity.

It worked the way it should.

I came into the picture when Nicole was just five. Samantha welcomed me as a co-parent and I was never viewed as the evil stepmother.

I thank God for that.

Nicole was bright and funny, artistic and outgoing. Then Samantha was killed in a car accident when Nicole was thirteen and all that changed.

She didn't become a bad kid, just a quiet one.

Our daughter Julie was six when Nicole moved in with us. With respect to Samantha I gave my all to Nicole.

Jeff never understood the 'change' in his daughter, I did. She lost her mother, a good woman, her best friend.

To compound that, Jeff had taken a teaching job in a school district outside of Los Angeles, California.

Our family was uprooted.

We found a great house, in a small town called Falcon's Way. A green spot nestled between the mountains and the desert. Population 2314. In a way it was a good thing.

A fresh start.

If I were to pin point a change in our relationship, it would be when the incident caused Nicole's downfall.

It wasn't when she got pregnant at eighteen. *That* I embraced. She did so well, never asked us for a thing. Maybe if she did, she wouldn't have gotten in trouble.

Two weeks before her son Tag's fourth birthday, Nicole was arrested for armed robbery. She was the driver in an incident that turned deadly. Two people died. The clerk inside the store, and the woman she hit when she drove off.

Life was turned upside down.

She had a child.

Nicole wasn't with his father, and the Los Angeles County Children Services gave us custody until she completed her incarceration. Then again, without parole, Tag would be a grown man when she got out.

Why didn't she ask for help? She said she did it for rent money. We didn't have much, but we would have done what we could. Jeff never forgave her.

One day he would have to, because Nicole never forgave herself.

I always wanted to tell him when he would ask the repetitive question on what he could do.

I wanted to say, "Make it right with Nicole."

But I knew he wouldn't. He would have to find a way to do so on his own.

Still, we lived our lives day to day, there was no rationale to separate, and I just constantly searched for reasons to stay together.

We ended up with a reason.

Not that Tag wasn't reason enough. He was. But any inkling to leave was tossed out the window when I found out I was pregnant. Intimacy was sparse and I could pinpoint the day we conceived.

It was a surprise. A result of delusion by wine. Too young to be a grandmother, too old to have a newborn. I was in the proverbial hard place. Even with Julie a couple years from college, I was going nowhere.

I had to find a happy medium because life, for as unfair and unbalanced as it could be, wasn't going to change any time soon.

At least that was what I thought.

TWO – ROUTINE

July 8

There was no drawn out trial, Nicole pled guilty and was sentenced to twenty-five years. Since she was moved to a state penitentiary almost a year earlier, it was my weekly routine, no matter the weather or circumstances, to go on a visitor day. I never missed a Sunday neither did Tag or Julie. I was grateful, and it was easier once the prison system switched Sunday visitor hours from eight a.m. to one p.m. That made things easier. Still, it was something that was part of our lives; everything else was planned around it. I was still trying to figure out how I wouldn't miss a Sunday when the baby came in three months.

I actually panicked about that.

More than anything I didn't want her to feel abandoned because of a mistake. One that she felt and regretted every day.

I liked the summers better because we didn't have to rush back. At the beginning of the month we stayed at a cheap motel after the visit and returned home the next morning.

Visit fifty-one would more than likely be the same as the previous ones.

This Sunday was no different. We woke up, rushed as we always did, downed a quick breakfast of cereal, and as a family, the four of us went to church. Every Sunday, I searched Reverend Ray's words for something that Jeff would hear as a sign to go with us. Each week I believed I heard something, but Jeff did not.

We filed out of the community church, and like every week, the young reverend imported to us from Ohio would wish us a safe journey, turn to Jeff and ask, "Will you be going?"

"Not this week, Reverend." Jeff answered, the same, never making eye contact. A quick shake of his hand and off Jeff went ahead of us down the steps.

We weren't a big town, one of those places everyone knew everyone's business. They all knew we went to the prison to see Nicole and that Jeff stayed behind.

By ten a.m. we were back home. I quickly made sandwiches for the trip and packed us a small bag. Jeff planted himself in front of the television.

What was going through is mind? Did he debate going? One day he would truly regret it.

"Jules, can you get Tag in the car seat?" I asked.

"Sure. Come on, Tag." She reached out her hand for her nephew.

I noticed her blonde hair was in a ponytail. "Hey, did you bring an extra band for your hair?" I asked. "Last time they made you remove it."

"Yeah. I'm ready this time." She opened the door. "Bye, Daddy. I love you."

"Love you too, sweetie. Remember I won't see you until Wednesday."

"We'll be back tomorrow," Julie said, with some shock.

"I'm filling in this week in Santa Ana."

Julie cringed. "Oh, that's right. Sorry Daddy."

She and Tag darted back in to kiss him goodbye. Jeff was very loving with Tag and Julie; it broke my heart that he just couldn't find it in his heart for Nicole.

After the two of them stepped out, I placed my hands on Jeff's shoulders and leaned down from behind him and kissed him on the cheek. "I wish you were going."

"I know you do."

"I'll call you when we get into the motel."

"Please." He grabbed my hand. "Be safe."

"You, too."

I tossed my purse over my shoulder, grabbed our brown bag lunch and moved toward the door.

"Tess."

I stopped.

"Try to eat. I'm making some extra cash from this teaching stint. Take the kids to dinner tonight."

"You sure?"

"Yeah. You're eating for two and when you do these trips, I know you barely eat for one."

"I'll do that. Thanks."

No sooner had I stepped onto the porch, Del Bender, my spry and friendly senior neighbor lifted his hand in a wave, while trimming the hedges.

I returned the wave and he signaled me to stop, held up a finger and went into the house.

The kids were already in the car, it was hot and I tossed my items in the car.

"Can I drive?" Julie asked.

"Honey, we are cutting it close."

"I know. I know. Please." She begged. "I'll be careful and I won't be too slow."

I was thinking about it when Del crossed our lawn holding a bag.

"Tess." He handed me the bag. "Mary made this. Some cookies. Maybe Nickie would like some."

"Aw that is really, sweet, please tell Mary thank you."

"Mom," Julie pressed. "Can I please?"

"The highway is dangerous. You're just starting."

"I'll drive until the highway. Statistically speaking, the chances of me having anything more than a fender bender right now are slim. Please?"

"Yeah, go on."

"Yes." She clenched her fist and hurriedly got the driver's seat, probably, before I could change my mind.

"Statistically speaking," Del said. "How many 'statistically speakings' do you hear a day?"

"As many as she can dig up on that phone."

"Don't think she makes them up?" he asked.

"No, she enjoys statistics. And I can bet she looked up the statistics of new drivers and accidents."

"Hmm." He grumbled. "You're a brave woman, there, Tess. I saw her pull out of the driveway. Statically speaking, she'll knock out that mailbox by next week."

"Probably. I'll let her drive until we reach I-10, then I'll take it. Give her a half hour of practice. Thanks again for the cookies."

Del nodded then peeked in the car. "Watch your left as you pull out, don't cut it too soon or you'll hit the mailbox again." He said to Julie, and then peeked in the back seat. "See ya Stevie."

Tag giggled and waved. Del was the only one who called him Stevie, refused to call him, as he put it, the baby name.

Finally we were all in and Julie backed out. As always, I held my breath, tensed up when I saw her cut the wheel too soon, and cringed when I hear the crack.

"Shoot." Julie gave me an apologetic look.

12

"I got it!" Del yelled. "Get going."

Julie looked out the window. "Thanks Mr. Bender." She cut the wheel, again too soon, hitting a curb shot as she straightened out the car and got on the main street. "He's so nice," she said. "Sorry about that."

"You're fine, just pay attention."

Three houses down the street, Tag said, "Sam is decorating again."

I looked at the house across the street. There was a giant flag in the front lawn and other Patriotic memorabilia decorated it.

"Looks like another antenna," Julie said.

"Don't look at Sam's house, just drive." I instructed.

"I like Sam," Tag said. "He's fun. He said he'll teach me how to shoot a gun when I'm older."

"Swell," I waved to Sam.

Sam was a nice man and Tag was always racing over to his house to talk. He was the neighborhood eccentric. His house not only screamed it was in dire need of repairs, but also it cried out 'American'. Sam, as a veteran, let everyone know he served his country. As did his father and grandfather.

He was indeed hanging another antennae or something like that on his roof. He had so many antennas and dishes, I worried his already failing roof would collapse. But Sam kept adding them.

Julie was too engrossed in watching him, despite my instruction to mind the road. She swerved once, straightened out, flashed me a smile and drove on.

I knew I was a glutton for punishment for allowing her to drive. Hopefully, we'd make it on time. At least when I took over on the highway, we stood a chance.

THREE – REGRETS

Julie was talkative. Not that she didn't talk a lot as it was. Julie loved to ramble. But on the trip, she was especially chatty. Her enthusiasm for life was amazing. She was the brightest in her class, and the most responsible teenager. I didn't get angst from her. I got a great friend, and a daughter who respected me as a mother.

Her hair was a lot lighter than mine, but she wore it the same style and length. Plain enough to pull off a clean cut look and just long enough to pull back. Julie didn't need make up, even though she wore it. I believed it was because she was insecure about her weight. I never saw an issue, I always saw the great child of mine. But kids were cruel. Julie had it tough. My heart broke for her so many times when she'd come home crying. Even as a teenager, she didn't have many friends. Nor did she ever have a boyfriend. She was a beautiful girl that, in my opinion, was going to soar when she grew up.

We had pulled over to our usual switch spot to change driving responsibilities. A truck passed us, causing my heart to jump. I hated pulling over. Even though I did so deep enough into the shoulder of the road, I worried about someone ramming into us. Especially with Tag in the back seat.

"Did you see that guy?"

"Which guy?" I asked, getting into the driver's seat. "Buckle up."

"I am," She fastened her belt. "The one in the passenger seat."

"I didn't look."

"You should have. He looked like one of the J's."

I hesitated before pulling out. "The J's?"

"Yeah, you know. They live down the street. Their mom and dad host the block party every year."

From the back seat, Tag said, "Josh and James."

"Oh." I sang out and pulled on to the busy road. "Okay, Josh and James Mason." I knew who she was talking about. They lived down the street and I remembered them when we moved in. They were funny, upbeat and always selling something when they were kids.

"I'm gonna marry one of them."

"Who?" I asked with shock.

"The Mason's. Probably. Josh."

"Julie, I think he's a little old for you."

"Right now," she said. "He's twenty-two. But in five years, it won't be that bad."

Suddenly Tag giggled.

"What's funny?" I asked.

"Julie will be one of the J's."

Julie grinned widely and turned back to look at her nephew. "Yes, you're right. Way to go Taggy. I'll be a J." She faced me again. "They are so cute."

"They're old for you."

"But they're cute."

I nodded. "They're cute." And they were. Neither of them were bad boys. They worked jobs. Wasn't sure what they did, but they still lived with their parents so whatever it was, it didn't pay much. "I just … I just always thought maybe Nicole for one of them."

Julie gasped so loudly, I thought she'd choke on her gum. "Mommy, no, you can't give Nicole to one of them."

"What's wrong with your sister?"

16

"Nothing is wrong with my sister, for them, she's wrong. They go to church all the time. We see them. And Nicole is …" She lowered her voice to a whisper, held up her hand to block her mouth and said, "Tainted." Julie pointed back to Tag.

"Oh, my God. Stop hanging out with Mrs. Bender."

"I like Mrs. Bender. Plus, she gave us cookies for Nicole. If you think about it, tainted or not, by the time, Nicole gets, you know, released … statistically speaking, one of the J's will already have been married and divorced. And more than likely, when she gets out, she'll not have an interest in men."

"Julie." I scolded.

"It's true."

"Statically speaking?" I asked.

She smiled and sat back. "Yep."

The Hideaway Hotel located about six miles south of the prison and just outside of Chino was our preferred location of lodging.

Stan the motel manager/owner was always a bright spot. He insisted that we check in before we went to the prison. Always fearful that there be some sort of riot, we wouldn't return and he loses the money from the room. I don't believe anyone was ever knocking people over to get a room there.

So, we checked in, and headed straight to the prison after dropping off our things in our room. It wasn't the best motel. It was far from it.

An "L" shaped, single story building with maybe fourteen rooms, at one time it was probably a great place to be. Affordable accommodation for traveling families of the past decades. Now it was an affordable place to stay for people visiting loved ones in prison. I was pretty sure it hadn't been updated since 1982.

We arrived at the prison with seven minutes to spare. Good thing, because they wouldn't let us in if we were late.

Miranda was a guard at the prison. A middle-aged woman who called me by my first and last name. "Tessandra Lordes. Good to see you. How's that growing bulge?"

Growing bulge. As if my rotund belly was a product of beer.

She seemed nice enough; then again, I wasn't a prisoner.

After checking in, we arrived in the visitor room. A big room, where everyone gathered with their family. Nothing was private. We were allowed to have one brief kiss and hug when we got there. I wished with all my heart, I could give my hug time to Tag.

He sat near as he could to Nicole. She looked good. Her long dark brown hair was shiny, and not pulled back. The last two times we visited, I worried. She looked pale and had been battling some sort of stomach flu.

"How's Daddy?" she asked.

Every visit she asked and every visit, I hated responding. "He's good. He's busy and …"

Nicole held up her hand. "Don't make excuses for him, Marmie."

Marmie.

That was what she called me for as long as I remembered. Out of respect for her own mother, she never called me 'Mom', so she grabbed the closest thing to it.

Tag called me that, as well.

"You got big," she said to me with a nod of her head to my stomach.

"Yeah, I think I popped this week. Still so far to go." I rubbed my stomach.

"Is he kicking a lot?"

"Oh, yeah. Maybe I just feel it more, because I'm old."

Then Julie and Tag started talking, I just sat back and watched. Nicole was absorbing it all. But she was doing something I hadn't seen her do in a while. Genuinely smile. Not a forced one or brief one, a genuine look of peace.

"You look good," I told Nicole. "It's good to see you smile."

"I got two bits of good news," she said. "Wanna hear?"

"Absolutely. I love good news."

"First … we got approved for a family visit."

Julie shrieked with delight, so did Tag, I was speechless. A family visit was something Nicole had to apply for. Since she had a son, she could get a family visit or at least apply for one every six months. They were visits that were in apartment style settings and the visits were for about thirty-six hours.

It would be our first one.

"When?" I asked.

"September. I'm so excited. You'll be really close to your due date though."

I waved out my hand. "Doesn't matter, you have a maternity ward here, right?" I winked.

Nicole laughed.

"And the other news?"

"I heard from the Watsons. Joel Watson."

My heart sunk. "What ... what do you mean, heard from him?"

"He wrote me."

Joel Watson was the husband of the young woman Nicole struck with the car. I saw him at the sentencing hearing and like he did with the news, he was screaming for justice. I couldn't imagine what this man had to say to Nicole. She sobbed and apologized that day over and over.

"What did he want?"

"Want?" Nicole shook her head. "Nothing. He wrote to let me know it was time to forgive myself, because he had forgiven me."

"Oh my God." Immediately emotions welled in my throat. "I'm happy for you. How do you feel about that?"

"Glad. Relieved. I don't know that I can easily forgive myself. I know I won't ever forget it or stop getting that knot in my gut when I think about it. I'll just learn to live with it. It makes it easier knowing he forgives me." She released a soft chuckle. "Funny. A man I don't know, a stranger who hated me, forgave me, when my own father can't."

"I'm sorry."

"No, one day he will. I believe that."

Quickly, I reached over giving a squeeze to her hand, and retracted before the guards saw. I wanted to repeat that whole cliché that it was his loss, not hers.

But that wasn't true. Not having her father's forgiveness or love was a huge loss to Nicole.

I then switched the conversation. Nicole was starting to get down, thinking about her father. Tag needed a good visit with his mother, and time was short. The news about the family visit was good. Plus, it gave me time. Hopefully, by autumn, when the visiting day came, Jeff would find it in his heart to join us.

FOUR – STALLED

July 9

Check out time was eleven am, and I had every intention of getting up and on the road by nine. What little items we brought were already in the car, and all we had to do was brush our teeth and go.

My body, however, decided it wasn't going to obey the agenda.

I pushed it; I knew it. The pregnancy was hard on me and would only get harder. I couldn't do the things I wanted to do. Even working part time at the grocery store hit me hard.

We had an early dinner the night before. Too early, by eight p.m., I was starving and since we got such a great deal on our dinner, I ordered a pizza. Tag was bouncing off the walls from all the soda and when Julie and I made the error of binge watching episodes from Season Two of Living Dead, Tag took it as a slumber party. I think he passed out somewhere during episode four.

I debated on sleeping. After all, the sky was getting light by the time I said, 'enough was enough'. Knowing that Jeff was out of town, I opted for sleep.

And didn't wake up.

Of course, the wakeup call never came. Not an unusual occurrence for The Hideaway. Often times I thought it was Stan's way of getting that dollar a minute from those who checked out late.

When I finally woke, and saw that we only had ten minutes until check out, I sat up in bed. "Shit."

My swearing caused Julie to immediately wake. "What's wrong?" she asked.

"We slept in. We have ten minutes. We have to …" I swung my legs out of bed and stood. When I did, I felt the pinching on the left side of my back. It caused me to pause.

"Mom? What is it?"

I exhaled through parted lips. "Just a pain. God, I hope it's not another kidney stone."

It felt like that pain and I was hoping it was just the way I slept. I got kidney stones and they were bad enough, having one pregnant would be worse.

Snatching up my clothes, I raced to the bathroom, instructing Julie, "Text your dad, tell him we got a late start."

When I emerged from the bathroom, I saw a puzzled look on her face. "What's going on?"

She held up her phone. "Text won't go through. We had a signal last night."

I lifted my water bottle, took a drink and grabbed my phone. "No bars."

"Wonder why."

I shook my head and then I thought about it. "It's the ninth." I cringed. 'Bet the phone is cut off."

"Mom," she whined.

"I know. I'm sorry. I'll deal with it when we get home. Go peek out the door to see if Stan is lingering."

"We still have five minutes." Julie walked to the door, opened it slowly and looked out. "We're good. I don't even see the maid."

"Oh, good, let's get out of here before he negotiates minutes with us." I pointed to Tag who was still sleeping. "Grab him, put him in the car. I'll be right out."

Julie obliged. I grabbed the small items in the room, including our bag of chips, since we weren't getting breakfast, and with one minute to spare, we were in the car and pulling out of the lot.

Stopping for a late breakfast wasn't an option, but lunch was. I promised Julie that we would hit Rose's Diner as soon as we got into town. I was hoping though, she would want carry out. Truth be known, I wasn't feeling well. The pain in my back came in cramping waves, my stomach fought nausea, and I started to sweat. I didn't need to be a doctor, I had experienced it several times before; I was going to be passing a stone. Of all times for Julie not to be a good driver, that pull over just off the interstate couldn't come fast enough.

"I have to pee," Tag called out from the back seat.

"Can you hold it?" I asked. "We're almost at the pull off."

"I have to pee bad."

"Well, listen to some music, maybe it will take your mind off of it." I reached for the radio and turned the knob.

Nothing.

I pushed the presets then hit scan and the numbers just scrolled through.

"Mom?" Julie asked with concern. "Why is there no radio?"

"I don't know." As if it would make a difference I kept hitting buttons.

"I have to pee."

"We'll stop in a minute," I said. Then it dawned on me. Was it my imagination or had we not seen that

24

many cars. The normal steady flux of traffic was reduced to an occasional car zipping by us on the freeway.

No. It was my overactive imagination. Everything was fine.

I shut of the radio chalking it up to being my car, and inwardly cheered as we drove off the exit. At a safe distance from the highway traffic, I pulled over, and put the car in park.

"Julie, can you grab Tag and take him over the hill to go?"

"Sure. You okay? You look pale."

"I'm not feeling well. It's a stone. I know it. You're gonna drive though, okay?"

"Yeah, sure." She stepped from the car and opened the back door, unbuckling Tag.

"Take him a good distance," I yelled.

"I know your fears. I will."

I watched as they stepped over the guardrail and then down the small slope. After checking my side mirror, I shut off the car and stepped out. Walking would help, move a little.

There was an unusual quiet about the day and I couldn't put my finger on what it was. I walked to the passenger side of the car, and glanced over the hillside at Tag and Julie.

When I turned, I heard the frantic beeping. It broke the silence in a frightening way. Looking to the road, I saw a pickup truck moving down the highway. Not super fast, but steadily, not stopping and he headed right toward me.

I was frozen in fear. It was something I visualized many times. The truck horn was steady, a warning of sorts and at the last second, I snapped out of it and moved quickly. It was just in the nick of time, too.

The truck swerved only a little, but enough to side swipe my car before it crashed into the guardrail.

Julie frantically shouted. "Mommy!" Surely she heard the crash.

"I'm fine!" I looked to my right to see her holding Tag on the other side of the guardrail. "I'm fine. Stay there." I held out my hand and raced to the truck.

The driver's side door opened and Josh Mason jumped out. The young man was hysterical and frazzled. "Oh my God. Are you okay?" He ran to me. "Oh my God, I'm so sorry. I don't know what happened."

"I'm all right. Are you hurt?" I asked.

"No. I don't think." He ran his hand over the top of his head. "I don't know what happened. I was coming around the bend and my truck just died. It died. It wouldn't steer or stop. It took everything I had … I'm sorry."

"No. No, honey." I reached to him. "No one was hurt. We just need to figure out how to get back."

Then from behind me, as if the accident never happened, bright and chipper, Julie blurted out like a teenager, "Oh, hey, Josh. How are you?"

Is she flirting right now? Right now? I thought, and then peered over my shoulder to face her possibly even scold her.

That was when it happened.

Everything brightened. A brilliant, blinding white light blanketed us, causing everything to appear polarized. At the same time a static and sizzle sound echoed across the valley. My feet wouldn't move and for a split second, I swore I couldn't breathe.

Josh's eyes widened as he looked beyond me. "Oh my God."

The sheer look of terror on his face, sound of his voice, told me, it came from behind me, probably west. Even though I was fearful, I spun to see.

The sight knocked me back and I immediately grabbed for Tag, bracing him in my arms.

I wasn't sure what I was looking at or what just happened. Was it a bomb? A meteor? I didn't know.

Clutching Tag and my daughter, pulling them close, I prepared to say goodbye to my life and everything that I loved.

It was the end. I was certain.

Whatever occurred in the distance appeared to have erased everything on the horizon and replaced it with what looked like nothing less than a wall of fire.

FIVE – ROLL OVER

Something clicked in me. Holding Tag and Julie, staring out at what I believed my destiny to die, a switched flipped.

It all happened in seconds, I went from resolving my life, thanking God for all he gave us, asking Him to make sure it wasn't painful for the children to screaming inside, 'I want to live!'

My fight to survive instinct kicked in.

If indeed that line of fire were to roll our way, the only chance we had was to take cover. Clutching Tag, I spun, yanked Julie and cried out. "Over the hill!" making my way to the guardrail. I knew the hillside wasn't that steep, perhaps if we ran down, it was our only hope.

Julie hurriedly climbed over, I handed her Tag, and as I raised my leg, that was when I realized, it wasn't as easy for me. It was a struggle with my stomach.

"Run," I yelled at her. "Take the baby, run, and get down.

From my peripheral vision I saw Josh, easily go over the guardrail, and before I knew it, stuck somewhere in a mid straddle, Josh hoisted me up and pulled me over.

When he set me down, I lost my footing and slid down the hill some, feet first.

The bottom wasn't that far, maybe thirty feet. A gradual slope, and as I reached the bottom, we all got down, staring up to the road.

Waiting.

Waiting for whatever would either rollover our heads or down the hill. I breathed heavily, scared to death, but refusing to show it for my family. The fireball never came. It was hard to gauge how long we waited, for all I knew it could have been only seconds. But long enough that Josh stood.

"Where are you going?" I asked.

"I have to see," he said. "If it isn't here by now, then it's moving slow. I have to see where it is."

"What if it's right there?"

"Then I'll know," he said and crawled up the hill.

"Why we hiding?" Tag asked me. "Are we playing?"

I glanced at Tag, then at Julie who was petrified.

"No, baby," I answered. "We're being safe."

"From what?" he asked.

How to answer? What to say? I just didn't know.

"Mom?" Julie looked at me, face red. "What's happening? Is it war?"

"I think so." Peering up, I saw Josh get to the guardrail and step over. Where was he going? What did he see?

I waited. Crouched down as close to the ground as I could get. My anxiety caused the baby to kick and kick again. Just as I reached down to my stomach, I got the gut wrenching thought, *'My God, if this is nuclear war, what about my baby?'*

"Here he comes," Julie said.

Josh came down the hill at a good pace and held out his hand to me. "Let's go."

I used his hand as leverage and stood. "What did you see?"

"I didn't see the fire. I did see black, possibly smoke, I don't know," Josh said,

Julie asked. "Do you know what it was?"

"I'd be guessing," Josh replied. "But it's out west. Could have happened close, far, perception could be off. But let's get off this hill and try to get home."

He was right. The best way to find out answers would be to get back to our town. It was thirty miles away. I could have been overreacting, it could have been just a gas explosion that was close. But there was no rumble, no noise.

We climbed back toward the roadway. Josh's truck may have been useless, but we still had my car.

SIX – ROAD HOME

Josh needed to get a few items from the truck before we headed back home to Falcon's Way. He retrieved a backpack, toolbox, bottle of water and other items from the cab of the truck. Just to be sure, he tried starting it one more time.

It never even made a noise.

While he did that I examined the sky.

Had I imagined the large wall of fire? Perhaps my eyes played tricks on me. Josh had mentioned smoke, and I did see a huge layer of black clouds forming further west. It was impossible to tell how far or how close. The fire was gone.

My car started without incident, and I didn't think about that at all. I just needed to get home. Something was happening and we didn't know what.

I inwardly felt that sense of urgency laced with fear. I tried hard not to project that to the kids. No longer did my side hurt or back. The flash in the sky was an instantaneous cure for my kidney stone. Or a temporary one.

Tag continuously asked what was happening and Julie started to sound panicked.

"Mommy, what's going on? I'm scared."

"I know, sweetie," I said.

Josh hopped in the front seat after tossing his items in the back of the SUV. "I didn't see any tire damage. You should be fine steering."

"Let's hope," I pulled out onto the road. "And your truck just died?"

"Everything, just died."

I reached for the radio. That was when it dawned on me. The radio hadn't worked all morning. "Josh, does your phone work."

"I wasn't able to get a signal. I was rushing, so I didn't think that much of it."

"What do you mean?" I asked.

"I hung out at a friend's last night, had too much to drink and slept in the pickup. When I got up, I just needed to get home because I was late for work. I tried to call my boss, but the phone didn't work."

"What about now?"

He lifted up in the seat to reach in his pocket. "Weird. It's dead."

"Dead?"

"Like no power at all."

I lifted my eyes to the rearview mirror."Julie, check your phone."

After a beat, she replied. "Dead."

Blindly, I reached for my purse and tossed it to Josh. "Look at mine."

"Want me to go in your purse?"

"Yes."

He undid the fastener and reached in. "Here." He pulled it out. "Dead."

"Shit." My foot moved to the brake and I slowed down to a near crawl, then finally stopped.

"What's wrong?"

"Something must have happened twice. Once early this morning, and then again just before we saw the flash. It had to have." I said. "We couldn't get a signal, we didn't see anyone. Now this. "

"What do you think it is?" Josh asked.

"I'm not an expert. I'm just gonna guess. Sounds like an EMP. Maybe two. I can't figure out why the phones lost signal first. That's the only thing I can think of."

"What is an EMP?" He asked.

"Electro mag … something pulse."

Julie corrected me. "Electromagnetic pulse. Seriously, dude, you really never heard of an EMP?"

"No, seriously," Josh said. "I don't pay attention to that science shit."

"It's history shit," Julie argued.

"Julie," I called her name. One minute flirtatious, the next irritated.

"Mom, it's just that anyone who ever watched a sci-fi movie, reads or passed science, should know what one is."

My daughter was a good student and a bookworm. It made sense that she knew.

"Okay," Josh looked back to her then to me. "Pretend I'm illiterate and tell me."

I explained. "It knocks out all electronics. Theoretically, what was running when it hit will never run again. Our phones were on, you were driving. Now they don't work. This car was off. It works. It's what makes sense."

Josh further questioned, "What causes it?"

I shrugged. "Lots. Not sure. I know a nuclear weapon does."

Julie added, "So does the sun. But the biggest classification is an X flare, and even the biggest really wouldn't do this. It has to be a weapon. A nuke."

"A nuclear weapon?" Josh said with a hint of sarcasm. "Did you see the size of that fucking fireball? That's one big bomb."

"Josh," I scolded, as if his swearing really mattered at that moment. "I'm not saying it was. Just guessing.

Can you think of anything else that could hit this widespread? You have a better guess?"

"Aliens."

"Oh, yeah, that's better."

"Getting back to Falcon is the best way to find out," Josh said. "Maybe everything is fine there and they are watching the news. Whatever it was, will be on the news."

I agreed and put the car back in gear and drove on the road. It was thirty miles to home and I would take it slow the entire way, just on the outside chance that whatever had occurred, happened again and I wanted to be in control of vehicle if it suddenly went dead.

There's something to be said about wishful thinking, hoping that something will change. The definition of insanity is doing the same thing over and over and expecting a different result. Under that definition, I was insane.

I checked not only my phone, but also the radio dozens of times in those first miles. I needed to hear something, know anything. My eyes shifted to the rearview mirror to make sure Tag was still buckled in, then Julie who had instantly calmed down. She stared out the window, biting on the nail of her index finger. She looked deep in thought, not crying or freaking out. In fact I was willing to bet she was thinking about the situation, wishing with all her might she could pull out her phone and hit the internet for research. She looked more 'together' than Josh. Had I not known my daughter as well as I did, I would have sworn she took a pill or something. Radio, phone, passenger's, continuously making sure my car hadn't lost power.

Between doing all that, I didn't look ahead.

"Watch out!" Josh shouted.

Instinctively, my foot slammed on the brake. What driver doesn't slam the brake, no matter what speed they travel when someone shouts out?

Right before me was proof enough why I was doing the right thing by driving slow.

Josh wasn't the only one to lose power to his vehicle. Typically, a vehicle would just putter out, slow down, but not when going down a grade with many turns.

The sight of the older model minivan sickened me, because I knew a minivan meant a family. It had rolled. From what I could tell, it hit another car, and probably flipped in the air before careening against the side of the hill.

Glass shattered everywhere; the car it struck was completely smashed on the driver's side. Groceries scattered about the road. One of them had just gone shopping.

My eyes were transfixed on the wreckage. I wanted to continue on, ignore it, more so because I was fearful of what I'd see.

With a hard lump in my throat, I squeaked out. "Please everyone check their phone to see if we can get a hold of 911."

Julie answered. "It's dead."

Then I heard Josh.

"Oh my God."

I looked over at him, his eyes widened then his hands covered his face and his head lowered.

"What … what … is it?"

35

"Up head on the road."

Don't look. Don't look, I thought. Then I did.

Ahead, a good thirty feet I saw the outline of a body. It was more than likely ejected from the vehicle.

My stomach knotted, heart beat fast, and some sort of adrenaline immediately kicked in.

I threw the car in park. "Julie, watch Tag. Josh, let's go." I opened my door.

"Mommy? What you are doing?"

"We need to see if anyone needs help."

"If they do … how?" Josh asked.

"I don't know. We're ten miles from home, the clinic is there." I stepped out of my car, paused and looked at the wreckage before me. Far enough away that I couldn't see any details, or any more bodies other than the one on the road. I could barely swallow, my throat was swollen from anxiety.

After we had stepped from the car, I looked over at Josh. "Check the car."

"Me?" He squealed in shock.

"You'd rather check the minivan?"

"No," he replied.

My first inkling was to move to the van, then I saw the body on the road more clearly. "Oh, God. Josh it's a kid."

I raced as fast as I could down the road, hoping the child was alive. The closer I drew, I saw it was a boy, he lay on his side, back toward me. He could not have been any older than eight or nine. He wasn't moving.

When I arrived at him, I swore he looked as if he were sleeping. On his side, one arm crossed over, the other extended. I dropped to my knees, truly afraid to get a close look.

My hand reached to his arm, and it was warm. I took that as a good sign at first, until I got a better look at his face.

While there was very little blood, I knew by the color of his face, the child had been killed. My face tightened up, my trembling fingers reached for his neck, seeing if I could find a pulse.

That portion of his body was cold. He wasn't warm from life; he was warm from the sun.

My insides twisted, turned and fought vomiting.

I didn't know the boy, but my heart broke right there for him. I couldn't help it. I started to cry.

I couldn't just leave him there, but I didn't know what to do.

"Dead." Josh called out. "The woman in the car is dead."

"Check the van."

"Are you serious?" Josh asked.

Hand still on the boy's body, I screamed. "Check the fucking van!"

"Fine."

On that road, I had to think. What to do with the child? How to move him aside or take him? Leaving him there wasn't an option. He was just a child.

"Man and woman in the van are dead," Josh shouted. "No kids."

No shit, I thought. *He's right here.*

"Josh, I have blankets in the back of my SUV, can you grab one please?" I requested.

Josh answered. I don't know what he said, I was too engrossed in that moment.

"I'm sorry little one," I whispered, to the boy. "I am so ..." Lifting my head, I saw the sickening sight of it. Off to the shoulder of the road, another ten feet ahead on its side.

A car seat. A bigger one, not an infant seat.

Oh, dear God, another child.

"Grab both!" I shouted for Josh, then stood and blinked hard as if to squeeze the tears out of my eyes.

What had happened? How and why did that minivan lose power at that exact moment on the road? The worst turn, steepest slope. Ten more seconds and they would have been fine.

I prayed that car seat was empty. That maybe it wasn't connected and that child stayed back from the shopping trip. I didn't run to the car seat, I walked with trepidation.

"Be empty. Be empty," I repeated softly with each step.

Just as I neared the back of the car seat, I saw not only a portion of an arm showing from the edge of the seat, I saw the abundance of curly blonde hair tainted red with blood.

That was it. That knot in my gut, rolled up my chest and shot from my mouth before I could stop it. My own child kicked in the womb, as if to let me know 'he' was still alive.

I didn't vomit much. Never in my life had I had a reaction like that. I couldn't look anymore. Even just a glimpse was enough to get me sick. I figured I'd go back, get a blanket and toss it over the seat before moving it.

After wiping my mouth with the back of my hand, I took a step.

Whimper.

I stopped. Froze.

Another whimper. One of those 'I am about to cry' whimpers. Immediately I spun around and zoomed in on the car seat, then I raced to it.

That portion of the arm moved outward then up and I lost all breath. The child was still alive.

It was hard to say if it was a boy or girl, the clothing was neutral color and covered in blood. The toddler had a deep abrasion on the forehead. I didn't have time to assess how badly the child was hurt. I just knew we needed to get help.

I shouted out, "He's alive!" and hurriedly grabbed for the seat. When I tried to lift it the little child looked at me and started to cry.

"It's okay, it's okay," I spoke soothingly. I wanted to take him out of the seat, but again, didn't know how badly he was hurt. The seat was heavy and awkward, but I lifted it, as I did, Josh headed my way.

"Here, I'll carry it," Josh said.

"Let's put him in the car, we'll get him to town," I said. We made the exchange, he handed the blanket to me, and then took the seat.

When he did, I saw the other child on the side of the road.

"Josh," I said. "We have to move the other boy. We can't just leave him there. Can you …"

"Yeah, let me put this one in your SUV," he said.

I nodded. My insides shook, hands trembled, the child was alive and that erased, a little, of the heartache over the other boy. Blanket in hand, I walked to the older child and covered him until Josh could move him. Turning, that's when I noticed. Julie wasn't in the car with Tag.

She was out on the road grabbing the groceries.

"Julie, what the hell?" I asked and approached her. "What are you doing?"

She had one full bag in her hand and was loading another. "You'll thank me."

"For what? Taking from a family that died?"

"They don't need it."

"Julie!"

"Mom, they had canned goods, box goods, and batteries. They were running, something happened."

"It doesn't make it right. Stop it."

She ignored me and kept grabbing things.

"Julie."

"Let me at least grab the water."

"No, you can't …"

"The child's in the car," Josh interrupted. "I'll move the other boy. What are you doing, Julie?"

She avoided answering him and grabbed more items.

"She's grabbing food from the road," I answered. "As if we're starving."

She turned and literally freaked out on us. In a way I never saw her act. "Something happened! The sky lit up. There was an EMP. These people were in a hurry. They were bugging out. Bugging out, Mom." She then called down and grabbed two bottles of water. "They knew something we didn't."

As if anything I said didn't matter, she continued. I returned to the car.

By the time I got there, the toddler in the seat was crying and Tag was holding his ears.

"Let's go home Marm." Tag said. "Please."

"We're leaving," I started the car, watching as Josh carried the dead boy over near the van. Instantly I felt guilty for leaving the child's body there, but there was nothing we could do. We had to get to town to get the injured baby some help.

I laid on the horn. "Let's go." I said, even though they couldn't hear me.

Josh raced back to the vehicle, and then Julie, after lifting one more thing and placing it in the bag returned to us.

She opened the back hatch, tossed in the items, then got in the back seat. "You'll thank me," she said.

I wanted to reply with 'I doubt it', but I refrained. I focused only on driving around the wreckage and getting to town.

SEVEN – TOUCHED

For those who had never heard of Falcon's Way, it was a great place to stop. An oasis out of nowhere when traveling the winding two lane route through the mountains.

It took a good hour to get to high tech medical care. Although Falcon Memorial was considered a hospital, I viewed it more as a clinic. A fifty bed facility with an urgent care and maternity ward. For things like broken bones, delivering a baby, minor injuries and the flu, they were hands down pretty decent. For more intricate illnesses and injuries, they sent you elsewhere.

I worried about our injured toddler. Would he get the care he needed? It really was the only option. We determined he was a boy because he wore blue pull-ups instead of a diaper. That alone told me he was between the age of two and three. He cried and whimpered. I made Julie constantly try to keep him awake due to the head wound. The poor thing. Even if he knew how, he wasn't speaking. I just wanted to cry for the family he lost and the life he'd never know.

The nice thing about our town was a person could walk from one end to the other in twenty minutes. More than likely they would know the name of every person they saw.

The plan was to walk. We'd head to the hospital, Josh would drop off me and the baby and he would leave to take Tag and Julie home. Then he'd check in with his mother and father. His family needed to know he was fine.

However we still weren't certain if we what experienced an hour before hand was an isolated incident or bigger than we wanted to admit.

Pulling around that last bend just before town, I saw the flashing red and blue lights of a parked squad car.

Josh perked up. "Police car is working. Falcon's not affected."

"We can tell them about the accident." I said and pulled toward town.

Patrolman Bill Stevens waved his hand out, flagging me down.

Hating to stop, I wound down my window. "Hey, Bill. I really can't stop, it's an emergency."

"Everything is, Tess," he said. "I'm stopping everyone."

"There was a big accident ten miles back on seventy-four," I said.

He nodded toward the front end of my car. "I see."

"No, not me. Another. Big accident. It's bad, Bill."

"We can't head out, Tess. Have to hold fort here."

I closed my eyes and nodded. "I have a kid in the back, he's hurt bad. Can I get through?'

He looked into the car. "Jesus," he commented when he saw the baby. "Yeah, go. Memorial is open."

Just as I was thinking, 'why wouldn't it be', Bill stopped me.

"Tess, listen. You have one of the few working cars in town. Be careful and protect it. Okay?"

I nodded, thanked him, and really didn't think about what he said. I pulled forward, aiming for the turn to the micro hospital two blocks away.

Julie must have. Because she asked, "Why didn't you find out what was going on?"

I looked at her through the mirror. "I don't know. But at least Falcon is fine, right?"

"No, I don't think it is," Julie replied.

"Me either," said Josh." He mentioned you had one of the few working cars. He's stopping people coming in. So he's protecting the town."

To me that was silly. Protecting the town from what? It was when I hit the turn for the hospital that I realized, Falcon was struck as well. The stoplights were out, a telephone pole was down at the bend and we were detoured around because fire fighters were battling a blaze at Greco Plumbing.

Julie was right. I should have asked. But getting help for the baby was foremost on my mind.

I picked up the speed to get to the hospital. Whatever event had occurred rippled at least as far as our town. That told me it was big. Bigger than a quick answer a police officer would be able to give. It wasn't going away and I'd find out soon enough what had happened.

My priority was getting the baby to the hospital and getting Tag and Julie home and safe. Everything else was secondary for the time being.

EIGHT – WAIT

Why I was expecting things to be different at the hospital, I honestly didn't know. The sliding double doors of the two story building were open. I suppose to allow sunlight in. Whether or not they had electricity or generators remained to be seen. Beyond those glass doors was dark. But people moved in and out, and a security officer must have thought my vehicle was a temporary ambulance, because when I got out and lifted the car seat, he said to Josh, "Is that it for drop off?'

"Yes, sir."

"Ok," He pulled out a notebook from his pocket. "There's a couple on fourth that need to be transported here, breathing problems from the heat."

"But I …"

"Thanks." He put away the notepad, placed it back in his pocket, and turned to me. "They'll see you inside."

Josh pulled away and I felt compelled to tell the guard, one of the few people in town I didn't know, that, "Josh was dropping me off. He's not volunteering. I don't want those people to go without help."

The guard looked at me. He was about the same age as Josh. "They won't. Josh will get them. I know him. He'll feel guilty and get them."

"As long as he gets my kids home first. Could you ..." I asked, gesturing to the car seat. "It's really heavy. He's injured and I don't want to move him."

"Sure." The guard took the seat and led the way into the emergency room.

There weren't many people there. Which was a good sign. It was dark sans a few emergency lights and lanterns.

I approached the main counter, and the car seat was placed on the floor by my legs. I felt bad, looking down to the little guy. He was sad, not feeling well, and I was certain like any child, he just needed held. But to me, he must have been injured because any child his age would be fussing to get out of the car seat.

"Tess," Carol, my neighbor was working as the admission's nurse. She said my name with shock. "You okay? The baby okay?"

"Yeah, yeah, I'm fine. We were coming back from seeing Nicole and we passed an accident. It was horrible. I found this little guy in his car seat. His entire family was … you know." I paused. "He was thrown. He's not crying, but I'm certain he's hurt. He's conscious and not screaming."

Carol came around from the counter. "I suppose you don't know his name."

"No, and he hasn't talked."

"Probably shock. Scared." Carol crouched down before him and checked him out.

"Carol, what's going on? Do you know?"

She shook her head and stood. "No, no one does. This all just happened about an hour ago. I mean the loss of power."

"Did your phones go down first?"

"No. In fact I was on the phone when it all hit."

Hearing her say that caused me to pause a moment. My phone wasn't working before the power went down. Confirming my original suspicion that two things had occurred and I was close to the first.

"They're saying …" Carol stood. "It was an EMP. But no one has been able to pick up any news, not from what I heard. Again, I've been here. I think his little arm may be broke."

I whined out a compassionate 'aw'. I felt really bad for him.

"I know he's not your responsibility, but can you stay with him until we look at him and figure out what to do with him?"

"Sure. Not a problem."

Carol lifted the car seat. "I'd take him out, but let's see what Dr. Stanley says."

I cocked back. "Dr. Stanley? He's here? He retired last year."

"He came in. In case we needed him. We did." She led the way to the back. The injured toddler totally jumped the line in the ER.

She brought us into Room Four.

I thanked her as she closed the curtain, and I faced the baby. "I'm sorry you're sick."

His little lips puckered and he started to cry. "Mommy."

"I know. I know." I moved closer, stroking his face. "It will be all right. I promise. You will get better."

He repeated 'Mommy' again and again. It hurt to hear him say that. Yet, he was speaking.

I did the soothing 'shh' thing, then asked. "What is your name? Do you know your name?"

He nodded.

"What is it?"

"Yee-am."

"Yee-am." I blinked. "Yee-am." The fast opening of the curtain caused me to jump. I spun to see Dr. Stanley standing there.

He wasn't old by any means. He retired young when the insurance companies started dictating what he could do. He was one of the last of his kind, a single doctor practice.

His blonde and gray hair was combed neatly. He seemed comfortable working, not stressed or rushed. "Tess," he said. "What's going on?"

"Accident on the road. I brought in the only survivor. I couldn't do anything for the others. Poor family is still up there. Just laying there."

"I'm sure authorities will get up there," He said. "So you have ... oh my God." Dr. Stanley walked to the bed. I guess I was blocking his way. "This is the Sanders child."

"You know him?" I spun around.

"I should. They moved in the house next door to mines about three months ago. New in town. Surprised you didn't see the welcome on the church sign."

"I did. But I hadn't met them."

"Poor thing," Dr. Stanley said. "I can't remember his name."

"Yee-am."

Dr. Stanley grunted at me. "Liam. Good Lord, Tess has it been that long that you don't remember child talk." He reached to unfasten the seat.

"He was thrown," I said. "I found the car seat on the side. I didn't want to move him in case he was hurt bad."

"Good thinking, but I think this little guy's injuries aren't life threatening. Just a gut instinct. His angels

48

were watching over him." He undid the fastener. "How are the kids? Tag? Jeff? How are they handling this?"

"Handling what? No one knows what is going …" And then I dead paused. Just stopped cold.

Jeff. Nicole.

It hit me.

I was so engrossed in all that was happening, I didn't think of them. I totally forgot Jeff was teaching out of town. Worse part was both he and Nicole were west, same as that fireball we had seen. That thought alone, immediately made me sick.

NINE – REAL WORLD

It was time for reality to hit me. I knew what I saw, experienced, and then I was so focused on getting home I didn't think about the bigger picture. Sure I asked, but I accepted the general consensus answer that no one knew.

Dr. Stanley said he was certain Liam had a broken arm. He didn't appear to suffer any serious damage, but they wanted to keep him in the clinic and watch him for a few days.

Then what?

His family was dead.

"They have family in Texas," Dr. Stanley said. "We'll reach them when the phones get back up."

"Will they?"

"I'm certain."

I said goodbye to Liam and told him that I would be back to check on him, as I was leaving, I paused in the room. "Doc, if it was some sort of bomb, is my baby gonna be okay?"

"I don't think it was a typical bomb, if it was a bomb at all. But that baby is fine. It has the best protection."

"What about radiation."

"If there was radiation, it's way out there."

I accepted that answer and took comfort in it and headed back home.

I'd be lying if I said I didn't hope Jeff was home. I did. The entire walk there I kept thinking that whatever occurred, it happened early and he never ended up leaving.

He was sitting at home with the kids; that was what I believed.

I ended up walking the entire distance home, it was uncomfortable, the heat increased and I could feel the sun beating on my skin. A couple blocks from home that kidney stone loosened back up and I could feel the cramping knot hit my back.

My street was a community of its own, a tight knit family and as soon as I turned the bend for my street, I was spotted and everyone flocked to me as if I were a celebrity.

They engulfed me and bombarded me with questions.

"What did you see?'

"I wanted to ask the kids, but I didn't want to scare them?'

"You saw something."

"You came from the west."

I couldn't answer, the questions rapidly fired at me. My line of sight drifted to Sam. He was in his yard, wearing some sort of garbage bag looking outfit that covered him from head to toe. He also looked as if he were searching for metal.

"What is Sam doing?" I asked.

"Being nuts," one of my neighbors said. "Come on, Tess. We can't wait for Josh to get back. He's been running your vehicle like an ambulance."

Swell.

Del Bender broke through the circle of people. He was with my neighbor from across the street, Larry.

Del said, "Tess, we're glad you made it back. What do you know about what happened?"

I shook my head. "Nothing. None of you know?"

Del replied, "No even crazy Sam hasn't heard anything on the multitudes of radios he has. At least he says he's not heard anything."

Larry was a bearded man who looked like a mountain man. When actually he was the mailman for twenty years. He said, "We've been in the dark, literally. All we know is the town went into full emergency lock down mode."

"What does that mean?" I asked.

"It means," Larry explained. "That deputy Bill Stevens came though here with a bull horn and the old squad car telling us until we knew what happened, we were under a martial law of sorts."

At that moment, Sam came into the circle and removed his gas mask and then hood from his body suit. "Clear. No radiation. None that I'm reading." He indicated to the contraption in his hand. "Doesn't mean it will stay that way."

"What the hell are you talking about?" Del snapped. "What radiation? There wasn't a bomb?"

"How do we know?" Sam said. "Power went out. In fact, transformers sparked, that tells me it was an EMP."

Del waved him off. "Doesn't mean a nuclear explosion. Could have been a fancy EMP type of bomb by the terrorist."

People in the circle scoffed audibly at that suggestion.

Sam added, "Okay, well what about the nuclear reactors all around Los Angeles? And us. They shut down that fast, there's been no cooling the rods, and radiation could and will escape."

"I'm sure they have backup," Del said. "Things will be back on line. Nothing exploded."

"Not true," I said. "Something did. At eleven, our phones had power but no signal. An hour and a half later, we had stopped to switch drivers and that's when it happened."

Everyone's voice merged as one.

Del held up his hand. "What happened? Then there *was* something?'

"Explosion. Fire. The sky lit up. I mean bright white. There were no winds. But I saw a fireball in the distance."

Larry asked. "Fire ball or mushroom cloud."

I shook my head. "Fire. Mushroom. I don't know. We ran for cover. But it looked like the sky exploded."

Del grunted out and tossed out his hand. "Goddamn North Korea."

"We don't know," Larry said, "But I can find out. First light I'll take the plane out. Fly out far enough to try to see. West? Is that right Tess?"

I nodded.

Sam spoke up. "What about radiation? You could be exposed if there's radiation."

"Chance I have to take. We need to see. If there's no news, we have to find out ourselves."

"How you gonna do that?" Del asked. "With Sheriff Stew having us on lockdown."

"He's not shooting down my plane. And I'm damn sure he wants to know too." Larry said.

"Still not convinced it was a bomb," Del stated.

My head spun. The voices flowed together in logical argument. Bomb. No bomb. Meteor or comet. Alien invasion. The theories flew along with more questions for me. I tried to answer theirs, now it was time for them to answer mine.

"Stop." I lifted my hand. "Has anyone seen my husband, Jeff? Is he home? Do you know?"

I wanted someone to say 'yes'.

But Del didn't give me the answer I wanted to hear. "Sorry, Tess. I watched him pull out just as the sun came up."

"Shit!" Sam blasted. "Shit!" He stepped back.

I looked at him curiously. "Sam?"

"Shit. The sun." And on that, saying no more, Sam spun and hurriedly ran back to his house.

TEN – COOL

Despite the fact that Del told me Jeff had left, I was still hopeful, that somehow his car just died a few miles up the road, and he returned home. That wasn't the case when I walked in the door.

Julia had closed the blinds to keep the coldness in, there were no lights, and I started to get worried. I went into survivor mode. Not that I am all that much of a survivor, but I do have that little door that opens up when something goes wrong. Three years earlier when we experienced an earthquake, I swore would never be in that position again. At least I would try not to. We had no electricity, no fresh water, our food supply was limited to what we could get at the grocery store, with cash. The Sheriff was tough, laying down the law on how much someone could buy. If he hadn't, many would have gone without, because so many people went into hoarder mode.

Not that I stayed in complete stock, but I had a shelf in the pantry just for emergency situations.

When I walked in my home, I was ready to engage with what needed to be done.

Julie seemed glad to see me. Though I wasn't gone long enough to be missed. She rushed to me and said, "How is the baby?"

"He's fine. They are keeping him."

"Then what?" Julie asked.

"I don't know."

"Are we taking him?"

"I doubt that. I'm sure, before long, the phones will be up, and they'll find his family. Dr. Stanley is working the emergency room, and knew the baby. His

55

name is Liam. So I'm really sure, it's just a matter of time."

"And he's not too hurt?"

"No, thank God." I said. "Where's Tag?"

"He's playing with his Legos upstairs. I left a little bit of the blind open so he could see. Mommy, it's still really hot. The thermometer out back says it's eighty-nine."

"I know," I said. "But the sun will go down soon and the temperature will drop. I hope. "

"What about the food?" Julie asked.

"Exactly what I was going to talk to you about. Come with me" I led the way into the kitchen. "I've been thinking about it. Grab a notebook. We're gonna do an inventory, start keeping track of everything we have, everything we use. We'll start separating the box goods, canned goods, and then we will determine what will last the longest."

"Do you think the lights will be out that long?"

"Let's not count on them coming right back. That way we're ready if they don't. Remember the earthquake? I wasn't ready. I thought the power would be back on in a day, if that. But it wasn't. We went a week without lights, and were scraping the peanut butter jar. I said never again. I meant it."

"What about the stuff in the freezer." Julie asked.

"We have the grill. We'll fire that up and cook what we can and that's what we eat first," I said. I started opening the cabinets for a full and good view. It was then I realized I hadn't gone shopping at least in a week. "Julie," I said. "Do me a favor, go and get every battery out of every device that you can find."

"Good idea mom."

I was even proud of myself. I was sounding kind of savvy about survival. But I wasn't. I just kept going back to that day, that week, without power and the following month that left us with limited resources when the earthquake hit.

By the time I started really organizing the items, Tag reminded me that we had not eaten yet. I planned to start the grill and make that package of hot dogs that was in the refrigerator. All perishable items would have to be eaten first. I figured the items in the freezer would last until they defrosted and then I would have to clean them out. However, with the way the weather was holding on, it was midsummer, the things in the freezer would thaw rather quickly.

Once Julie returned and could keep an eye on Tag I went outside to cook. They only took a few moments and while cooking them I realized how hungry I was. We devoured the dogs.

After lunch, I examined the batteries Julie gathered. She had them in a plastic bag and set them on the counter. She tossed a few strays down stating she wasn't sure if they were any good.

Then she said something that clicked with me, "batteries will be hard to get. If the power stays out for too long, people will kill each other over a single battery."

Kill each other.

In that instant, following her comment, I was thrust into an instant panic. Out of survival mode sort of and into panic mode. When faced with extreme situations, people will take extreme measures. Suddenly, I started thinking about my neighbors in a different light. The people in our community. I knew them. A little differently at times because I knew them from the view of a grocery store checkout woman. I had worked at Monroe grocery store in town since we moved to Falcon's way. I did so up until I got pregnant with Baby X. I knew what people bought. I knew the shoppers that went once a month at the beginning of the month, I knew those who didn't buy much, and only went when they needed something. I knew those never bought enough food and those who bought too much. I knew those people and when they would run out.

Del's wife Mary was always in the store. Of course, no matter what she came in for, two of the items always included a pound of margarine and bottle of ranch dressing. I suppose coming in three times a week and getting margarine and ranch dressing she was either making some sort of bizarre recipe or has some sort of fetish for buying them. I imagined she had an entire cupboard filled with ranch dressing.

Mary and Del would not be desperate. I believe with how wonderful a cook Mary is she sure could find a way to survive on margarine and ranch dressing.

Melissa Owens was another story. Her husband was constantly out of work from being fired or drunk on the job. Melissa always told me her marital woes while I was ringing her up. She also purchased her groceries with checks. No one used checks anymore. Mr. Monroe would always hold her check for a day or two, instead of using automatic authorization, which told me Melissa pushed the envelope of living paycheck to paycheck. She never bought extras. In fact, she got barely enough. How much more food she could have gotten for the kids if she didn't have to buy beer for her husband. He wasn't a nice man. What would he do when they ran out of food? Nothing himself, but I could see him sending Melissa to our house to cut our throats for a box of cereal.

They weren't getting mine. With my mind swimming with thoughts of my desperate neighbors breaking down my door and trying to slaughter my family over a few bits of Ritz crackers, I turned to Julie and said, "They'll kill for more than batteries. I have an idea. I want to leave no more than a couple days worth of food up here. Take the rest down and hide it in Daddy's marijuana room."

"I'm sorry. What?"

"We have about enough food for three weeks, I figure. But we have to be careful. Up here we have the perishable things like cereal, and fruits and vegetable. And a couple of the canned goods. Someone breaks in here, we don't want them to think we're stashing. The rest we'll take the rest downstairs to his marijuana room."

"I got the part about the food. Daddy has a marijuana room?"

"Well yeah. You kids didn't need to know. But Daddy likes to smoke the weed."

"Daddy smokes?"

"Yeah, but, it's not like he does it and enjoys it. He has a predisposition to glaucoma, and he wants to cut it off at the pass."

"Mom, you're not that dumb."

"No," I said. "Neither are you. Your father is a pothead. Always was, always will be." That made me pause. I hoped with all of my heart even as silly as it sounded, that Jeff would continue to be a pothead. If he was, he was still alive. "But we need to do this. It's a great room. No one knows it's there."

"Um, yeah. I didn't know. And I've lived here all my life."

Her curiosity was piqued, I could tell. She was still in a state of shock learning about Jeff.

We gathered up everything that we wanted to stash, and while Tag was occupied, Julie and I went downstairs.

Jeff's marijuana room was quite inventive. Originally it was a large walk-in closet with a single door. Not one of those fancy sliding doors, just a normal door. Jeff took off the doorknob, placed a faux bookshelf over the door, filled it with books that nobody wanted to read, and used a fake copy of the hardback version of War and Peace as the door handle. No one was the wiser.

It was a great little room. Eight feet long by about six feet wide. In there, Jeff had a small end table, his father's old reclining chair, a TV at the other end of the room, and his game console. There's no ventilation whatsoever. Which probably explained why Jeff was always so stoned after leaving that room.

I laughed at first when Jeff told me what he wanted to do with that room. I was laughing no more. Not only was it a great place to stash our food, Jeff also hid his gun box in there. The lock box that held the two pistols he got from his dad. That room, besides being Jeff's stoner haven, would and could be our safe haven. Not only was it a place to hide our food, but a great place to hide period if we ever needed to retreat.

◇◇◇◇

The temperature hovered above eighty and stayed there all night long, giving no relief whatsoever even after the sun went down. Tag finally fell asleep. He had a hard time and complained about the heat. Plus, he asked about Jeff and his mom. I didn't know what to tell him. I could sympathize with him all the way around. Especially with the heat. I had two furnaces burning. Mine and the baby's. I was absolutely miserable and stripped down to a light T-shirt and a pair of shorts. I didn't show my legs often but at that point I didn't care. I stepped outside on the porch to get some air and that's when I noticed. The entire street was pitch black dark except, for Sam's house. One window exuded light. Not the dull or dim type of light you get with a candle or lantern, but full-fledged bright light.

While the rest of us were scourging for candles, Sam had power. He had power?

I told Julie that I would be back and that I wanted to speak to Sam. She thought that was a good idea, but I didn't know why she would think that. As I crossed the street, walking toward his home, it hit me. I didn't think much of his odd exit from the earlier conversation. That was just Sam. He was always eccentric. Yet, he ran away suddenly as if he had known something, and combined with the fact that he had power, my crazy neighbor, who was always prepared for something had me thinking. What did he know? Was he indeed prepared for this, whatever it was?

The doorbell didn't work, so I knocked lightly. I didn't want to wake him if he was sleeping. Although, I don't know if you could sleep with that bright light on. A few seconds later Sam answered the door kind of surprised.

"Hey Tess."

"Hey Sam. You got a minute?"

"Yeah, come on in."

"Thanks".

Sam asked, "Is everything okay?"

"Yes, I just have a few questions to ask you." I stepped into his house.

"Close the door, don't want to let the cold air out." Sam said. "I only have another twenty-two minutes with this thing on. I want to enjoy it all."

I didn't know what he was talking about until I stepped from the sweltering heat into his living room. It was an ice box. So cold I was willing to wager I could see my breath.

"Seriously?" I said with sarcasm. "The whole town is dark and you have air conditioning?"

"It's crazy I know. But I'm gonna enjoy it is long as I can. Have a seat."

I did. I plopped down on his sofa with a sigh of relief. "Oh my God. This feels so good in here. I'm dying."

"Well I'll have it going every night for about two hours until the generator runs out of gas." Sam said. "I'm using that to recharge my batteries, and try to find out what the heck is going on in this world. I know the heat is bad. I think it's gonna get worse. Don't know how you're gonna handle when it keeps going on for months and you're at that due date of yours."

"Months? This can't go on for months. Surely, the government…"

"The government?" Sam chuckled. "Don't count on the government. Seriously. We have to assume, that things are bad, Tess."

"You know something, Sam?"

"Not yet." Sam said. "But I'm trying. Fortunately some of my electronics survived because well, I heard about the sun releasing some sort of coronal mass. That happens a lot. And all my radio buddies said to stick one of my units in the Faraday Cage. In case you don't know what one is, it protects from the EMP. And the things that weren't running, thankfully they ran again. So I'm hoping, my buddies out there on the airways, and others like me, are just taking a moment to get things back up and running. I don't think the government is one of them, Tess. Honestly, I don't. "

"When will you know?"

"Couple days. Figure that's how long it'll take for the satellite signals to reflect enough for us to somehow make a connection. We'll get the answers. We will."

"Thank you."

"Is that all you wanted? "Sam asked.

"Actually, I came because I was curious to as to why you have power." I said. "But now I have something else to ask you. And it isn't just about what happened."

"What is it? "Sam asked. "Are you asking if you come over and enjoy the cold? Anytime you want…"

"No, Sam, seeing all this, and hearing you talk, I have a question. What can you tell me about survival?"

"Can you be more specific?"

"Everything. I need to keep my family safe and alive," I said. "If this is something big, and long-standing, which by your attitude, it seems like it is, I need to know what to do. I need to do things right. Especially…" I paused a moment and swallowed. "If Jeff doesn't come back."

"I can help you." Sam pointed to his own temple. "I'm a vat."

"I believe that."

"Well," Sam exhaled with a smile. "At least, I'm glad to hear you aren't like the others n this neighborhood, and think I'm that crazy, whacky, neighbor guy."

"To be honest, I did think you were crazy," I said. "But I don't anymore. Please help me."

Sam just stared at me. And then he smiled again. I didn't think he was crazy anymore. Not that I thought he was insane in the truest sense of the word, I just thought he was very eccentric. Now I viewed him differently. I viewed him potentially as my own personal survival encyclopedia. How could he not be in the midst of a blackout, a major event, heat wave index skyrocketing, I was sitting in a home with ice cold air conditioning. No, Sam was not only my new friend, he could very well be my family's salvation.

ELEVEN – EXECUTIVE ORDER

July 12

Three days.

I gave myself three days before I fell into despair. Then as if my subconscious was already waiting, on the third day, I opened my eyes to feel the physical pain of heartache.

Jeff hadn't come back.

Nicole was out there, near whatever we saw light up the sky.

Half of my family were more than likely gone.

The previous day my mind was so preoccupied with them, looking out the window, hoping to see or hear from them, that even the horrendous pain of my kidney stone was tolerable. It was nothing compared to how I felt when I thought about the loss of my family.

I had visited Baby Liam three times at the hospital. He developed a fever, but Doctor Stanley said the he'd be going home soon.

Where exactly home was, remained to be seen.

Tag slept in bed with me, his little body was drenched from sweat. I was too, it was hot. I couldn't wait for my hour at Sam's, and I'd slip over there and just sit. Medication, I claimed for the baby.

Lying in bed, running my fingers through his damp hair, I was hit with an overwhelming sense of sadness. What would I tell him about his mother? What would he remember?

I just stared at my sleeping grandson, his still eyes, and perfectly pouting lips. What was going on? There was no news, nothing was known. Was this now life or would things go back to the way they were? It was in that quiet, sad moment, that a 'thumping' caused me to jolt.

It came from downstairs. At first I filled with excitement, thinking Jeff was back. Until I heard more noise and male voices. I couldn't make out what they were saying.

"Oh my God," I jumped out of bed, my first thought was to call for help. There were looters in my house. But since there weren't any phones, I raced quietly to the bedroom door, and locked it. I planned on yelling out the window, but that would draw attention.

Then I thought of Julie. I was keeping myself and Tag safe, yet, she was probably sleeping and unknowingly a possible victim.

No. I had to protect my family.

Keeping them protected ran though my mind after my talk with Sam and I did what he suggested. I placed the revolvers, in two different places, high, out of Tag's reach, hidden, loaded but with the safety on.

One was in my closet.

The noise and voices continued below, and I retrieved it. My plan wasn't to go downstairs and pull a Clint Eastwood, it was to remain vigilant and ready by the bedroom door and if they came up, I'd shoot.

Unlocking the door, I quietly slipped from the room into the hall, stood near the steps and flipped off the safety. Surprisingly, I wasn't shaking or scared.

Then I heard the one male voice. "Leave that cup of cereal, and instructions. Did you mark everything down?"

"Yeah, Sheriff."

Sherriff?

When I heard that, I immediately recognized the voice and barreled down the stairs.

Sure enough, before they saw me, I saw them. Sheriff Stew was in my kitchen with what I guess was his homegrown posse. Officer Steve wasn't there. All my cupboards were open.

"What the fuck?" I blasted, charging into the kitchen. Then I don't know why, I raised my gun.

Melissa Owens' husband, Chet, was there. How'd I know he'd be a looter? It took food to get his lazy ass out of the house. And the Sheriff, too?

Chet backed up with a "whoa."

"What are you doing in my house?" I asked. "I won't hesitate to shoot."

"Now, Tess," Stew said. "You'd be breaking the law and you'll only get one good shot off …."

"Then I'll aim for you," I lifted my aim at Stew. "Bet me Chet and Garret here run."

"I may," said Chet.

"Chet." Stew scolded.

"Just being honest," Chet said. "Look Tess, I'm only helping. I was drafted. Trust me I wouldn't do this. But he's making me cause of my size.'

Chet was a big guy, tall too. "I call Bullshit," I said. "And I will shoot. You're in my house and …" arm still extended aiming, I peeked in a box. "You took my fucking food. Leave, right now and bring back my water."

"Can't do that," Stew said. "This is the law. We ran around with the bullhorn yesterday letting everyone know to turn in their resources, you didn't."

"I had no idea what the hell you meant. And the day before you were running around telling people not to leave town. Who listens to you?"

"Everyone but you and Crazy Sam."

I shook my head. "You have no right."

"We have every right," Stew argued. "To take everything you have in this house. Food, water, batteries, every resource."

"What is this some sort of Stew power trip law?"

Stew shook his head. "When was I ever mean to you? Never. This isn't a Stew Law, it was a presidential law enacted years back. Don't believe me, go check the police station we have the law printed for folks like you."

"What law would say you can go into people's homes …"

Stew cut me off. "Executive Order of National Defense Preparedness. Under section 801, it gives Homeland Security and its local representatives the authority to seize all resources in the best interest of the community in the event of disaster. This is in the best interest. In my town one person won't starve while the other has plenty. Everyone will get the same. It's what we have to do to make sure there is no looting, that we all eat and survive. You're lucky." He waved a finger at me. "This works for you. You have a day's worth of food at most. Let's go boys."

"You can't do this," I growled. "Someone has to stop you."

Stew spun on his way out of the door. "Who? There's no government reaching out. No answer out there, for all we know we are the only ones left and we have to work under that assumption. I don't want to hear anymore from you about it, Tess. Be glad. Distribution registration starts at noon. We'll have everything accounted for by evening and start distributing. For now we left you enough food for the morning."

As I lowered my arm in defeat, Stew reached out quickly and took the gun from my hand. "We'll take this as well."

"Are you fucking kidding me?"

Then they barged out.

Taking my things.

They took all but one jug of water, all of my batteries, most of my candles, everything but one cup of cereal, a can of beans and ten crackers. I raced about the house making a list of what all they did take.

My ibuprofen, cough medicine, they had gone through my entire house and taken what they deemed resources. I wanted to scream. I was enraged. How dare they not only take my family's survival, but protection as well? Or at least they think they did.

Why my stuff? It wasn't like I was a prepper or anything like that, I was a normal every day woman and mother. No different than anyone else.

They took everything to make sure everyone had something. It wasn't fair.

I peeked out the living room window to Sam's house. I wondered if they went there first or at all. I didn't hear any shots, surely Sam would have fired at them. Sam's home looked undisturbed. In fact, I was looking to see if Stew and the posse were anywhere else on my street.

Just as I spotted them going into a home five doors up, there was a knock at the back door.

"Oh, so now you're polite," I griped, making my way to the kitchen door. "Now you'll knock. Did you forget something?" I grabbed the doorknob. "I suppose you want to claim the baby in my womb!" I blasted as I opened the door.

"No," Sam answered. "Not even if you're offering. You can keep the child," He stepped inside my home. "I work best with loaners, like the video stores used to do." He closed my kitchen door. "That's why I borrow Tag."

I looked down to the mug in his hand. "Is that coffee?"

"It is."

I took the mug. "I'm having a hell of a morning."

"I bet. Me, too. I just came to see how you handled it."

"Not, well," I replied. "I almost shot the sheriff."

"But you did not shoot the deputy."

"Huh?" I looked at him confused.

"Shot the sheriff. Didn't shoot the deputy. A song."

I shook my head.

"Too early, I guess or you're too young."

"Both."

"How you holding up?" Sam asked then reached for the items on the counter. "I see they left you more than they left me."

"Can you believe this?"

'Yeah, good thing you reminded me about that law."

"What are you talking about?" I asked.

"The law. That's what you were alluding to when you said you hid your supplies, right? I mean, that's why I hid mine."

"No. I was thinking of looters. I didn't know about the law. Although. Same difference."

"In Stew's defense," Sam said.

"He has no defense."

"Listen." Sam held up his hand. "We have a town. Two thousand people. Some, they don't have enough food in their house to get them to tomorrow. Others they have plenty. Are you gonna share your food when a family runs out."

"No. Absolutely not. No. It's to keep my family alive."

Sam nodded. "And Stew knows that is the general thinking. As a whole, this town has plenty to survive until a long term plan is devised. So he was taking the whole and dividing it equally."

"That is such a liberal way of thinking."

"It's survival, and he wants his town to survive. So he invoked the law."

I tossed out my hand. "It sucks. We don't know how long this thing will go on. He's certainly not winning next election. He's not getting my vote."

"Tess. There's not gonna be a next election. This world is different now."

I took a big swig of the coffee and handed the mug back to Sam. "Do you know something? Did you hear something?"

"Not anything. But I got static."

"Okay."

"I had dead air up until this morning. Someone is bouncing signals out there, I just got to catch it. And …. Larry went out this morning on the plane. Stew released the fuel for him to do so."

"So we'll at least know something soon."

"We'll have a good idea what's going on out west. And maybe find out what that flash you saw actually was. In comparison to the whole world, that's not much."

Wrong. My husband and daughter were west of Falcon's Way. More than anything, I needed to know. Contrary to what Sam thought, my entire world was west of me and knowing what happened to them was all that mattered.

TWELVE – HIGHWAY

I passed the stone. Although I didn't think that would help my mood. Two hours after Sam left, my stomach pains grew worse. So much so that Julie urged me to go to the hospital. I knew I'd be fine. Sweating profusely, I moved about, until finally I knew I'd pass it.

I did.

At least the pain from that took my mind off of the fact that I hadn't heard from Jeff. Where was he? I prayed he was somewhere safe. And Nicole, that prison was solid concrete. Was she still there? Was the prison intact?

Until Larry returned, I was still in the dark about what it was we saw.

I felt better. My stomach was bit queasy and I attributed that to not eating. The heat didn't help, last I looked the temperature was ninety and it was still early.

About noon, Josh Mason stopped by to check on us. I was grateful for that.

"She's sick," Julie told him.

"I'm fine. And I'm glad you're here. I want to head to that distribution registration. Can you stay with my family?" I asked him.

"Mom," Julie whined. "I don't need a babysitter."

"He's not a babysitter," I told her. "It's added security and protection."

Julie quietly laughed. "It's Falcon's Way. Nothing bad will happen here."

"Let's hope, you're right. I'll be back."

"Mom, you sure you feel okay to go?"

"Yes. Josh, do you mind?" I asked.

"No, go on. I have nothing else to do."

73

"Thanks." Then I instructed Julie. "Keep an eye on Tag. I'll be back."

Truth was, I didn't know when I'd get back. The note on the table said distribution was at Monroe grocer and I decided to walk there. I didn't need 'community' supplies, but I was going to claim mine anyhow. Even if it was only to get back my own food.

As soon as I stepped outside I noticed it. There was a weird color to everything. Stepping off the porch, I moved to the walk and peered up at the sky. A thin haze, almost smog hovered in the sky. To me, that explained the heat. The smog acted like a lid, keeping everything down and tight. I wanted to go back in my house and ask Josh if it had been like that all day, but decided it was something I could ask him later.

"Weird isn't it?"

Del's voice startled me and I spun to see him standing in his yard.

"I'm sorry?" I asked.

"Weird." He pointed up. "The sky. Awfully smoggy. I hope Larry is alright. I heard him fly out a couple hours ago."

"Hopefully he didn't have to land," I said. "I'm heading to distribution. Are you going?"

"No. Stew said because of our age we don't need to register."

"Lucky you." I took a step to leave then noticed. Del didn't look well. His skin was pale and he had a heavy layer of sweat on his forehead. "Are you all right? You feeling okay?"

"No. Heat is getting to me. House is just holding in the heat and pretty soon, there'll be no shade." He gave a twitch of his head to his tree.

The leaves were dying.

"Oh my God. This heat is killing everything."

"We need rain."

"That's not happening," I said.

"Well with this sky, you don't know."

I commented on how he was right, told him if he needed anything to let us know. And walked off. It took everything not to tell him about Sam's air conditioning, but it wasn't my place to spill Sam's secrets. I would, however, speak to Sam about letting them cool off.

As I walked to town I pondered the distribution set up. Would I have to wait in line? Would it be organized or screaming for help?

With all the homes, all the food, could they keep track of everything? I hope for speedy and orderly, but I knew that wasn't happening.

Three blocks from town, people ran by me. They held arms full of supplies. They raced down the street.

Another block, I heard gunshots.

Not much farther it was evident that Sam's perfect, equal society was a dangerous attempt at a humanitarian pipedream.

The sleepy, peaceful town of Falcon's Way erupted in chaos and rose up against the establishment. Well meaning or not, Stew and his band of Merry Men were outnumbered by the angry, hostile mob that broke the lines of distribution, crashed into Monroe's store and proceeded to strong arm those in charge and take what they could.

It was mayhem, and all I saw was disruption. No one attempted to stop them.

Total chaos. People were behaving mindlessly and violently. It wasn't safe. Bottles were thrown, furniture busted and not only Monroe's window, the other shops as well.

Right then and there, I realized Stew not only took a portion of my food, he took a portion of my security. I wasn't high and dry, but how many others in town now were because they entrusted in their fellow neighbors to follow the rules.

They would starve and struggle because of the selfish acts and desperation of people that they sat next to at church.

The cliché 'Dog eat Dog' held true in Falcon's way. I was down a week's worth of supplies, and by the looks of things I wasn't getting anymore. What I had hidden surely wasn't enough to last long term or until I came up with a plan.

My mind spun and so did my body as people blasted by me, knocking into me as they took off with food. Where did they think they'd go? Stew knew every person. Once he regrouped, he was going to go after those people and I didn't want to be seen in town.

I also needed to get my SUV hidden or at least disabled.

Being one of the last working cars in town, I was certain that my vehicle would be a next target.

Heading back home, I thought about Josh and maybe he knew something I could do to the SUV.

Del spotted me and called out. "You're back fast."

"People broke through distribution and looted it."

"Already?" he asked.

"Yeah."

"Oh My God. Is there anything left? Any water?"

"Probably not."

His hand went to his head and he sat down on his porch step. "We have nothing. He left us nothing. How am I gonna feed my wife? Where we gonna get the food from?"

"You had nothing stashed?" I asked.

"We gave him all we had. We might as well have just thrown it on the street."

My eyes widened. "Don't worry, Del. I have an idea."

"You know where to get food?" he asked. "Water?"

"I may." I raced back inside my house. Tag greeted me bright and cheerfully, and in my rushing, I blew him off. Then I stopped. He was clueless about the world gone mad, and it wasn't fair to him to dismiss the only bright spot of my day. I backtracked, kissed him and then continued on my plight.

"Mom? What are you doing?" Julie asked.

"Distribution was looted. People went nuts." I opened the hall closet. "I have an idea. Josh, stay with the kids, lock the doors." I not only grabbed the old green duffle bag from the closet I retrieved the revolver.

"Are you going looting?" Julie asked.

"You can say that." I rushed to the back door.

"Mom! You can't."

"I'll be fine. I'll be back."

Josh said something, so did Julie, but I kept going. The SUV was parked out back, and I would hide it in the garage when I returned. I was certain there wasn't enough of a posse to cover every street out of town, and I took the back way east out of Falcon, backtracking on dirt roads, and taking the long way to Mountain Highway.

It had been three days and chances were my shot in the dark would be a miss. But I had to try.

Fifteen minutes to bypass town and ten minutes on the winding mountain road. I expected it to be gone, for Deputy Stevens to have sent someone to the scene.

But no one did. It was still the same. The smashed white can and rolled minivan were still where I last saw them. So was the body of Liam's brother. Only it wasn't covered any more. Birds had found their way around it, removed the blanket and were boldly feasting on the remains on the little boy. They didn't even stop when I threw rocks at them.

When I stepped from my SUV, I had to pause, turn my head and vomit. My stomach churned and fought further regurgitation. I wanted cry out, and I felt a tremendous amount of guilt for leaving the child's body there.

It was too late now.

My plight wasn't to witness the crash site again, it was to get what I could find. No one bothered to come to the crash site, so no one saw what was up there.

The multitudes of canned goods, bottled water still littered the highway. With the open duffle bag, I proceeded to try to collect what I could. There was so much stuff. They had either just gone shopping for the month or like Julie said, knew something and were making a quick escape.

I was opting for the shopping. Most people left Falcon's way to hit Big Sam's wholesale, and the giant can of Big Sam's applesauce told me my guess was probably right.

It was in the middle of that highway, sun beating down that I heard the sound of the twin-engine plane.

I paused in my collecting and looked up to the sky. Sure enough Larry's red plane cut through the smog. He was safe, alive and returning.

As heartbreaking as it was and daunting, I remained on task and would do so until I grabbed every single item that I could.

78

That highway not only afforded me the chance to get food for my family, being there gave me first sight of Larry's return. Soon enough I would be getting answers. At least I hoped.

THIRTEEN – SPORADIC

The fully stuffed duffle was wedged behind the front seats, packed tight on the floor and covered by a blanket. The few straggling items I tossed in the back. I hated the fact that I had to drive around Falcon's Way and come in on Mr. Wesson's property, but it was the only way not to be seen by Stew or the town's people.

I had been gone nearly two hours and it was twenty minutes since Larry flew overhead. By now he either was just landing or leaving the small airport or with Stew. I would have to rely on Larry directly or even Sam for my information. Once in the car, I downed one of those bottles of water, the heat was unbearable. My hair and clothing were drenched with sweat and I hated consuming a whole bottle but I had to think of the baby. I was still feeling the after effects of that kidney stone.

I had water hidden and collected quite a few bottles on the highway. Del and Mary Bender were forefront on my mind as I drove back toward town. Before talking to Larry, I had to get water to them.

They weren't young, the heat had to be hard on them.

Middle of my drive back, I noticed the temperature reading on my dash. It told the outside temperature. I couldn't be right. I chalked it off to the vehicle baking in the sun, because there was no way it was one hundred and twenty degrees.

I wondered about town and if Stew initiated order. While I wholeheartedly disagreed with what he did, his intentions were good and the people that went nuts, in my mind, committed a worse wrong.

On the last hill into Falcon's way just before I'd turn off, I saw the smoke rising from town. It lifted high in the air and mixed with the lingering smog.

Swell, I thought, the town was on fire.

It really wasn't, but without water, how long would it be before it got out of control.

How could people do this to their town? It was only a few days; to be so desperate that fast.

I made my way around the outskirts, through Wesson's property then hightailed it by way of side streets home. No one saw me coming, and I sped into the back yard, got out of the car, opened the door to the garage, and pulled in.

I didn't realize how heavy the duffle bag was until I tried to pull it from the back seat. In my near seven month pregnant state, the bag, secured in tightly was an impossibility. I wondered if Josh was still in the house. I hoped he was. I needed him to do something to the truck. Render it useless but with an easy fix.

I had commodities, the working vehicle, food and water.

After forgoing the duffle bag, I raced in the house through the back door.

"Mom," Julie rushed to me."Where have you been? I was worried."

"I'm fine. I got supplies."

"Good but …"

My eyes shifted to Josh who walked into the kitchen, ignoring Julie, I turned to him. ."Josh there's a duffel bag in the back seat, can you grab it? Julie, there are items in the hatch, I need you to get them. Then Josh, you need to disable the car. I can't have people know it runs."

"Absolutely," He answered and walked out the back door.

"Julie" I faced her. "When we get the supplies inside, we take them downstairs. I need to get a care package together for Del and Mary. In fact maybe we should ration for five instead of three. Include them."

"Six," she said.

"Six? I'm sorry?" Before she could answer, I saw him in the doorway. Little Liam. "He's here?"

"Doctor Stanley said they closed the hospital. Didn't know where else to take him. I said it was fine that he stay here. You're not mad."

"No. Not at all. Did he say why? I mean, why they closed the hospital."

"No, he didn't. But statistically speaking, sixty-three percent of hospitals only have enough emergency power to run three days..."

"Is he speaking?" I looked at Liam.

"Oh, him. I thought you were talking about Doctor Stanley. Yeah, Liam talks now. He's chasing Tag trying to hit him with that cast."

"Good. We need the boys happy. We'll make some food in a few minutes. Go take care of them, I'll help Josh."

"Are you sure?"

"Yes. Go." I knew Josh was handling the heavy stuff and made quite the ruckus when he carried the bag inside.

"Where do you want this?" Josh asked.

"Take it downstairs," I told him.

"What's in it?"

"Food." I reached the screen door.

"Mom?" Julie called out. "Where did you get the food?"

"You don't want to know. But let's say, it was your idea." Saying no more, I pushed open the screen door, walked to the SUV, and grabbed the scattered items from the back. Josh and I passed each other once again.

"I'll take care of disabling the SUV now," he said. "Then what?"

"Pull the garage door closed." The items teetered in my full arms, and I made my way back to the kitchen, dropping everything on the counter.

I grabbed two bottles of water, and decided, I'd ration the food later, but getting water to Del and Mary was most important.

Julie was with the boys in the living room and I informed her where I was going and that I would be right back. She tossed another of her 'statistically speaking' facts at me that I was increasing my chances of heat exhaustion. I stepped out of the house on to the porch; the sky was growing more eerily green. And to toss even more confusion into the weird happenings, I watched the Snyder Family, all four of them, walk down our street pulling supplies in a wagon.

Where were they going?

Putting that out of my mind, I walked across the yard to Del and Mary's home.

The front window was open and the door closed.

I knocked.

No answer.

"Del. Mary?" I called out. "I have water."

I knocked again. Still no answer.

Figuring they probably went into town to get supplies, I put the water between the door and screen door, and left it there. The storm door didn't close all the way, but Del and Mary wouldn't be long, town wasn't that far.

Turning to go back to my house, I saw yet, another odd sight. A young couple, they were new in town and I wasn't sure of their name. I saw them at the fireworks the week before. They were on bikes, peddling down my street, both of them bogged down with huge hiking backpacks.

My eyes shifted, the Snyder's were at the end of the block.

Where were they going?

Ready to pass it off and go back to my house, I then noticed Sam stepping from his house. He waved to me then jogged over.

"Where you been?" he asked.

"I went to get supplies," I replied.

"Were you looting?"

"In a sense, but not from anyone who needed things. Why?"

"The kids were looking for you and …" Sam paused in speaking, and turned his head.

Wondering what captured his attention, I too, turned to look.

Not just a few, but several people, families, walked down my street. They resembled a pilgrimage. They all carried backpacks, pulled wagons, the Stone family pushed a Monroe shopping cart loaded with items. They moved at a steady pace, focused and not saying a word.

"What the hell?" I looked at Sam. "Where are they going?"

"Out of town. Prematurely, I'd say."

"I'm lost. What do you mean?" I asked.

"You don't know?"

"Know what?"

"Larry came back."

"I saw him fly overhead."

"Word got around fast."

"About?" I asked, then paused. "Oh my God. What did he see, Sam?"

"He came back and …" Sam hesitated, took a long blink, and then looked at me. "I think you need to hear it from Larry."

FOURTEEN – MOVING

I was never one to take in strays, yet there I was with another child. Liam was feeling better and was loud. Tag had reached the end of his patience and just wanted to play by himself.

"He's not very nice, Marmie," Tag said.

"He's a baby."

"He's mean."

"He's not mean, he's hyper."

"What's that?"

I pointed to Liam who ran about the first floor of the house in circles. His cast held high and he screamed as he ran, too.

"I'm getting a headache," Tag complained.

"Me, too." And I was. Only I believed mine was caused by a number of things. The heat, stress from waiting on Sam to bring Larry, and I was pretty certain, I had a second stone, or I didn't completely pass the first one. The pain in my back had returned and a knot of nausea hit my stomach.

I kept looking out the window. More people walked down the street, from what I counted it was close to forty. My street was the direct route out of town. It was probably was what happened to Del and Mary. I hadn't seen them and they hadn't returned. They got the news, whatever it was and high tailed it out.

Julie didn't ask and I didn't tell her about Larry. I figured why add another person to the neurotic list. When I had the facts, I'd share them. What exactly the facts were, I didn't know. I just hoped to find them out before Josh returned. Surely, he'd find out the second he went home.

I was angry with myself because when I was out on Mountain Road I never looked west toward the sky. I didn't think about it. My focus was on getting that food and getting back.

About the tenth time of trying to be inconspicuous and peering out the window, I saw Sam and Larry heading down the street.

Not wanting to hear anymore from Julie about my going in and out of the house, I snuck out. After all, how long would it take?

'What did you see Larry," I'd ask.

He'd answer.

And I'd go back in.

Larry and Sam were headed toward my walk when I stepped out and I cut them off at the pass. If people were leaving town, I didn't want to scare Julie or Tag.

Larry looked worse for wear. He appeared frazzled and worn out. I suppose he was bombarded with questions, and I was only compounding to that stress.

Arms folded tight to my body, I approached them. "Hey, Larry."

"Tess," Larry said. "I saw you up on old Mountain Road at that crash site today. What the hell were you doing?"

"Was that where you looted?" Sam asked.

I groaned and waved out my hand. "You saw me?" I asked Larry.

"I wasn't that high, I could spot that blue colored SUV anywhere."

"What's going on, Larry? What did you see? Why are people leaving?"

"I could only get so far west," Larry explained. "Saw the biggest lingering black cloud I ever seen in my life. It was moving, but slow. But it was huge. Darkened everything below it. It went as far south as I could see, so I headed North, Was able to catch the end of it about hundred miles up and could see beyond."

"Is that cloud coming here?" I asked. "Is it weather? A storm?"

Larry shook his head. "Wasn't getting any electrical disturbances. It was a cloud. Debris I guess."

"A nuclear cloud," I gasped out. "It's coming then."

Sam held up his hand. "He didn't say it was a nuclear cloud. But it probably is coming here. Unless the winds shift, which I doubt. It's held back because we got some out of season Santa Ana winds."

Larry added, "It's keeping that at bay, like everything else."

"Everything else?" I asked. "Like what?"

Larry hesitated and then looked at Sam before he answered. "Fire."

"I'm sorry. What? Fire? Like wild fire?"

"Like nothing I have ever seen. I don't know what caused it, but it's like one big inferno below. It's higher than most trees and just engulfing everything in its path."

His words made me stumble back. "Oh my God."

"It's moving slow," said Larry. "But I'm flying out again tomorrow to gauge the speed, maybe it's stopped. Who knows? I'll know more tomorrow."

My hand shot to my mouth and then it slowly lowered to my stomach. "When it happened, I saw a fire ball that took up the whole sky. I thought it was an explosion. It disappeared."

"Probably whatever caused it, erupted upwards then just started burning," Larry said. "We're guessing. We're in the dark in more ways than one, and if that cloud gets here, we will really be in the dark."

"So that's why people are leaving?" I asked.

Larry nodded. "They aren't chancing waiting on me and what I find out tomorrow."

"Then we should plan on leaving," I said.

"If that fire keeps moving our way. Yes." Larry said. "I can't see anything surviving that."

Upon his words, just as he spoke them, eerily it happened. Like some sort of sign. The first hit my arm, then a second smacked against my shoulder. I inched back to see what was going on, and another hit my forearm. All around me were the sounds of deadened thumps. One after another. Hitting the ground, cars and houses.

They fell fast and furiously.

I peered up, that was my mistake. No sooner had my head tilted back, the carcass of a lifeless bird smacked against my face. I screamed, brushed my hand over my nose and jumped back. The back of my shoe stepped on one.

"Holy Mother of God," Sam gasped and shielded his head. "What the hell is happening?"

There was no answer, no explanation, no escape. Steadily, they fell by the hundreds, if not thousands. As if God Himself, declared the avian species to be instantly extinct, and in midflight they just dropped.

It didn't stop and for at least three minutes it rained dead birds.

FIFTEEN – PILES

I believed there was no way we were the only ones in town pushing dead birds off to the side. Raking them into neat piles to be collected later.

Apparently, our section of town was hardest hit. Every neighbor that remained was outside trying to clean up the mess. It was horrifying that they fell from the sky, but even more frightening trying to determine why.

Having their dead bodies just laying there wasn't healthy for any of us. Especially in the heat. It took only minutes and the flies arrived.

Larry stated he was heading into town to try to get some large black bags from the fire department. It was safer now, the uproar and chaos ended when the distribution and store were nearly depleted of supplies. Suddenly not only did people have what they wanted, they were taking it with them as they left town.

There were a few items remaining and Sheriff Stew was closely guarding them. He'd had this big plan to save the town and I imagined his spirits were as empty as the town surplus.

My pile of birds grew and as I wiped the sweat from my brow, I saw Tag emerge from the house.

"Oh, whoa, look at all the dead birds." He bent down.

"Don't!" I yelled, dropped my rake and raced over. "Don't touch the birds." I pulled his hand away.

"Why is he dead, Marmie?"

"I don't know."

"Why are there so many dead birds?" he asked.

"I … I don't know. They just fell from the sky."

"Did they forget how to fly?"

From behind me, I heard Sam blurt out. "Jesus. The kid is an Einstein."

My mouth dropped open in offense and I spun. "Don't make fun of him."

"I'm not. I love Tag." Sam walked over. "He brought up a valid reasoning. Birds navigate by magnetic pulls on the earth. Whatever is happening could have just screwed them up."

"But made them just fall?" I asked. "No. No, they'd fly in circles or in no order. Something killed these birds."

"Look at his eyes," Tag stated.

I peered down. Tag was squatting curiously by the body of a bird.

"Tag," I warned.

"He's right," Sam bent down. "The legs are swollen and purple. The eyes look like their bulging out."

"So every bird is sick?" I asked. "Seems a bit farfetched."

Tag stood and walked to another bird. "His eyes are big, too," He turned. "This one too." "Stop!" While I thought it, it wasn't my voice that called out. It was Sheriff Stew. I turned around to see him walking down the street with Dr. Stanley.

"Step away from the birds, Tess," Stew said. "Grab the boy and get him away. In fact …" He raised the volume of his voice. "No one touch a single bird. You hear?"

"We can't just leave them on the ground," I argued.

Dr. Stanley then added. "Well you can't touch them. Getting near them isn't good."

Sam asked. "What's going on? Is it the bird flu?"

Dr. Stanley shook his head. "We don't know."

"Seems like an awful lot of birds to just drop dead with the bird flu," Sam said.

"There are many types of viruses birds carry, and some that are transmittable not only to humans but from humans. It's a chicken or the egg sort of thing right now," Dr. Stanley said. "These birds were sick when they died. And we just got about two dozen people in from the highway that were making their way east. Most them are sick with some sort of flu. So don't …" He looked at all of us. "Don't touch anything until we know what is going on?"

Fire burning out west, a looming cloud, birds dropping from the sky and sick people coming from the highway. Finding out specifically what was going on wasn't going to be easy. There was no answer to be found. In my mind, the simplest answer was. Things were just falling apart, we were at the end, and there was nothing we could do.

SIXTEEN - SMELL

There were no men and women in yellow biohazard suits and masks, no one in protective gear came for the birds. Stew and Dr. Stanley didn't want us to touch them, yet there was no answer on what to do with them.

They were left to rot. Alone on the road or in the piles that we had gathered.

No more news made its way to us regarding the people that came from the highway. Admittedly, I didn't seek out answers. My focus was on my family. There was a slight dip in temperature, but the house was still really hot. Unbearable actually.

Liam had no problem falling asleep. Julie was bored. I told her to start getting things ready to pack and go. She was unmotivated.

I didn't know when we'd leave, but it would be soon. The problem I had with leaving my home is we hadn't a clue what we were traveling into. What if there was nothing east? My imagination took off and I envisioned a globe of fire and we were the only speck not in flames.

Perhaps if I knew what caused the flames I would be more logical in my thinking.

Where we stood there was no television, radio, internet or phones. No means to reach the outside world. It was a black vat.

James Mason already left town with his girlfriend and his parents planned to leave in the morning. Josh wanted to stay back an extra day or two to see what was happening. As a mother I couldn't see his parents being very happy about that. But I was glad he wanted to stay back with us. Not that I wasn't capable of caring for my family, but in my pregnant state I wasn't as strong as I wanted to be. Especially with my kidney stone battle, which I was feeling more as the night moved in.

I knew it was cooler outside, but the stench of the baking and decomposing birds was too much to open the windows. Josh brought up a point.

"You'll get used to the smell. Trust me," he said. "Open the windows, let some cooler air in."

"I don't think I'll get used to it."

"Yeah, you will. You'll adjust, I know."

He must have picked up on my quizzical look. Although I didn't try too hard to hide it, I was a bit confused by his confident statement about smells.

He twitched his head once to the left, almost as if uncomfortable and said, "When I was deployed …"

"Deployed? Josh, I didn't know you were in the service."

"Reserves now, but yep. I was. The deployment was not a war thing, it was a police action. Let me tell you something, this weather has nothing on the Middle East. Anyhow we were on a convoy when we ran into an old mine or something. Whatever it was caused our truck to flip. One of our guys, Stanford, was hurt pretty bad. The radios weren't working, and I stayed back while Joel walked for help. It took five days for a search party to find us. Joel never made it and Stanford he died like two hours after Joel left. The only shelter we had was the overturned truck, sitting against it. Five days in the sun …. Anyhow, as long you don't remove yourself from it or get too far away, you get used to the smell. Even when it's that bad." He cleared his throat. "That's why I said, open the window. You'll adjust."

"Open the window," I told him.

I don't know what I was expecting. Maybe instantaneously, following Josh's story, I would be okay with the smell. I wasn't. The second the foul stench blew in, my already heightened sense of smell slammed into high alert. It caused my already weakened stomach to churn and I rushed to the bathroom.

It wasn't any better in there. We were rationing water and had one good flush a day. The second I lifted the lid, I was exposed to the day's waste and I added to it when I up heaved every bit from my stomach.

A burning sensation seared across my stomach to my gut and I fought the wrenching. My stomach, wanted to win that battle, twisting and turning and pushing.

I fought it and won.

My system calmed down, I poured a gallon of water into the back tank and flushed.

There was a gallon of clean up water on the floor, I poured some in my hand and splashed my face.

"You okay?" Josh asked from the other side of the bathroom door.

"Yeah." I replied with a gag.

"Here." The door opened and a shirt extended in. "No disrespect to Jeff, okay, please don't take it that way. I grabbed one of his tee shirts, and doused it with his cologne. It's ripped so it'll tie around your face. Like an outlaw from the old west."

I could smell the cologne as soon as he extended that shirt into the powder room. Then I didn't smell the cologne, I only smelled Jeff.

"Give … give me a moment," I took the shirt and closed the bathroom door.

Instantly, right there at that moment, my heart broke. My throat tensed up and the muscle spasms carried to my jaw forming a huge lump in my throat.

I had thought of Jeff, but I also had been trying to be so strong. The second I held his tee shirt in my hands and brought it to my nose, I collapsed. Back against the door, I slid down to the floor.

"I'm sorry, Jeff." I whispered at such a low level, my voice cracked and disappeared every other syllable. My mind drowned in a silo of guilt. Why didn't I tell him I loved him before I left? Why didn't I tell him, despite everything, I still cared? He tried so hard to keep our marriage alive and I never returned anything to him. It took until he was no longer in my life for me to realize how wrong I was, selfish. How much I did love my husband. It was too late. He left that day never knowing... "I'm so sorry." Not wanting anyone to hear me, I brought his shirt to my face and on that bathroom floor I muffled the sobbing for my lost husband.

Sobs that just didn't want to stop.

SEVENTEEN – SWEAT

After what seemed an eternity in that bathroom, I pulled myself together, splashed my face again and opened the door to find Josh was seated a short way from the bathroom.

"You all right?" he asked.

"Yeah. Just had a moment." I sniffed. My nose was clogged from crying, smelling wasn't that much of an option. Still, Jeff's shirt hung like a thick scarf around my neck and close to my chin.

"You're allowed, you know."

"I'm allowed to...what?"

"Have a moment. It's okay."

"Thank you. But my family doesn't need to see me having moments." Just as I finished saying that I saw Tag at the end of the hall.

"Marmie, tell me a story, please."

Josh stood. "I will. I know you go visit Sam for the hour."

I was about to accept his offer then I noticed Tag. His hair was soaking wet from sweat. "You know what? Maybe Tag would like to visit Sam with me tonight."

Excitedly, Tag nodded.

"I can tell you a story there," I said. "Josh, are you going home? Or staying."

"I can stay with Julie a little if you want."

"Please, thank you." I walked to Tag and extended my hand. "Let's go. Sam will be so happy to see you."

"You think it will smell there?"

"I think it smells everywhere." Holding Tag's hand, I looked over at Josh, mouthed the words, 'Thank you' and walked from the house.

As soon as we stepped out we were pelted with that smell. I took the shirt and placed it over Tag's mouth. We headed down the walk when my next door neighbor, Bill called out.

"Evening, Tess," he said, standing in his front yard with a shovel.

"What's going on, Bill?" I asked.

"Berch died, don't know what happened."

Berch was their retriever, a good dog, so friendly with a calm demeanor. Having been over ten years old, he was a huge part of Bill's family and life. It was sad news.

"The dog died?" Tag asked sadly. "Aw."

Bill nodded sadly. "Maybe it's for the best. The heat probably got to him. So, what are you doing up this late, young man?"

I answered. "He's hot, he can't sleep."

"Why don't you let him dip in the pool? Millie is back there. I keep it covered during the day, to keep out the sun, and none of the …" he pointed to the dead birds. "…hit the water. Go on. It's not cold but it will cool you down."

Tag looked up to me with his big brown eyes. "Can I, Marmie?"

With a heavy sigh, I looked across the street to Sam's. The blinds were closed so that told me he hadn't started the generator yet. Thinking about it, wetting him down then taking him to Sam's would give him a solid relief filled night from the heat. I would even dip my feet. The temperature was still high eighties.

"You know what, Bill, thank you. He will."

Tag excitedly jumped and hugged my legs. Sam's could wait, the swim was a nice idea and it couldn't hurt.

EIGHTEEN – GUESSES

It was amazing what a five minute dip into a pool did for Tag. The water wasn't cool, not at all, but compared to the outside air it was heaven. I kicked my feet in the water sitting on the side of the pool while Tag waded in water that came to his chest. Eventually he went under to soak his hair.

Millie didn't swim, the older woman only sat in the water. She said, "I'm enjoying this. Make sure you cover the pool each night."

"What do you mean?" I asked.

"Bill and I are leaving in the morning. You heard Larry, he said what's out west."

"What's out west, Marmie?" Tag asked.

"Nothing, Tag," I answered and turned to Millie. "Be safe."

"You aren't going?" she asked.

"Oh, we are. Probably in a day or so. Pushing the safety timeframe I suppose," I said. I didn't want to tell her I wanted to wait until most of the town had left simply because I had a working vehicle. The last thing I wanted was to drive with a steady stream of residents escaping town. Not after how they reacted to the food distribution. If they looted from the law, sure someone would have no qualms over taking my car.

I wasn't the best of company, not feeling well and depressed over thoughts of Jeff and Nicole. After several minutes and some chat, I could hear the hum from Sam's house and headed that way with Tag. My evening cooling salvation awaited and on this day, I needed it.

◇◇◇◇

Sam gave a strange examining look to Tag when we arrived at his house. I thought maybe it was because I brought him over, then I realized that wasn't it. Tag was always at Sam's house before everything happened.

"What did you do to him?" Sam asked, closing the door after we walked in. "Toss him in the water heater?"

"No," I said with a slight chuckle. "He was sweaty and hot. I let him jump in Bill's pool."

"The pool," Sam stated.

"Yeah."

"Hmm."

"What's that supposed to mean?" I asked, walking into his living room. I sighed out when I felt the coolness of it.

"The pool. It hasn't been filtering water for days."

"I could smell the chemicals."

"The birds fell today."

"He said he keeps it covered during the day."

"Hmm," Sam repeated.

"What, Sam?" I sat down. "Don't make me paranoid."

"Nothing." He waved out his hand. "You don't need the paranoia. At least you don't look like you do."

"Gee, thanks." I instructed Tag to sit next to me.

"You look drawn," Sam said.

"I had a moment tonight about Jeff."

"Ah." He tipped his chin. "You sick, kid?" he asked me. "You look pale?"

"I am. I've been battling kidney stones. And I have one that just won't pass."

Sam whistled. "I had a kidney stone once. Worst pain I ever felt. Some say it's worse than birth."

"It's not quite that bad, but it's bad." As I said that I felt the pain to my back, it pulled across my side and shot down my thigh. I jolted.

"You sure you're okay?"

"Yes." I snuggled with Tag. "Better now."

Tag looked up to me. "Tell me a story now, Marmie?"

"In a little bit, Tag." I stroked his wet hair. "We're visiting Sam."

"You can tell him a story." Sam walked to the radios. "I'm only playing."

"I kinda like chatting with you, Sam."

"I'm sure tonight's conversation will be censored." He looked at Tag.

"To a point," I said. "Heard anything?"

"Nothing. Larry is going back out again. We'll know more tomorrow."

"What about the folks who came into town?"

"That …" Sam held up a finger. "I did hear about. So far about three dozen have come through."

"Did anyone say what they saw? What happened?"

"Not right now. Half of them kept going, the other half are down and out until they get well. Some sort of bug."

"Did Dr. Stanley say anything?"

"Haven't talked to him. I asked if it were radiation."

"Why would you think that?"

Sam shrugged. "Because the sun is a big generator of radiation."

"You still think this was the sun."

"Absolutely, or a star gone nova. Thing is by the time we see a geometric storm, it had already happened thousands of years ago."

I squinted my eyes at him in curiosity. "Geometric?"

"Yeah, I think that's the term, it's like a big old blast coming at the earth."

"I didn't think anything like that could make it through our atmosphere."

Sam shook his finger at me. "Smart lady for a woman who is barefoot and pregnant half the time."

I laughed. I knew he was joking. "I read things on the internet. So this geometric thing. Can make people sick?"

"Well, it's more the gamma ray burst that will come with it."

Tag sat up. "Gamma ray. That's what hit the Hulk."

"Yep." Sam said. "Radiation." He then waved out his hand. "Of course, don't take what I say for gospel. I'm putting bits and pieces together from memory and I can be way off base. Still, I'm thinking radiation made these people sick."

"If they came from the west, and that was it, then if whatever is moving this way, it can make us sick, too. Right?"

"More than likely. I mean, what else would cause it?"

"What about the birds?" Tag asked. "They were sick."

I looked at Sam. "Could the birds have made people sick?"

"Yeah, or vice versa." He rubbed Tag's head. "Man are you smart. When I was a kid …"

A blip of static from the radio caused Sam to stop. He spun to face his set up.

Another hiss.

"Shit." He raced over and took his seat.

"Sam?"

He lifted one hand to silence me, then raised the microphone calling out. "This is DX6675. Blackstone. Anyone there? Over."

Hiss.

He repeated. "This is Operator DX6675. Blackstone. Repeat anyone there? Over."

A few seconds went by and more static. Sam wrestled with the tuner. And before long bits and pieces of a voice emerged.

We all squealed with delight.

Sam continued to twist the controls and try to tune in the voice. He said he'd keep trying and wouldn't give up.

Although over the course of my time at Sam's house nothing intelligible came through. Still it was a voice, calling out from somewhere. Even with the ratio of static overwhelming it, I took it as a great sign.

We were not alone.

There was at least an answer.

Someone else was out there alive.

Maybe, just maybe they knew what was going on.

NINETEEN – DISCOVERY

July 13

It hit me faster than I expected. The overwhelming need to vomit when I opened my eyes in the morning. For the first time, I didn't feel the effects of the heat; I was too busy focusing on keeping the contents of my stomach down.

The remainder of my water was on my nightstand and I sipped it, trying to keep the twitching to a minimum. I didn't know what caused the instant upset stomach, but I wanted it to stop.

Tag slept peacefully and right next to me. His hair wasn't soaking wet as it usually was, he was under the sheet instead of over it.

Had the temperature actually dropped? The thought raced through my mind, and then I saw the amount of light seeping through the blind. It had to be before six am, it wasn't quite fully light out.

My stomach calmed and I decided to go back to sleep when I caught glimpse of the wind up alarm clock.

9:55.

Had it stopped from the night before or was it that late? The darkened sky meant one thing … rain.

To say I was excited at the prospect of rain was an understatement. I quickly stood from bed and paused at the pain in my lower back. That kidney stone was close to making its way out; I knew it.

I walked to the window and peered out. The sky was overcast and there was without a doubt more of a green tint to the day. No sooner had my fingers released the parted blinds, I hear the sound of the twin-engine plane. Larry was flying out. We'd get some news, hopefully good news.

With the sun not beating down, the temperature would be tolerable.

I hoped.

After kissing Tag on the forehead I grabbed my water, used the last few drops to brush my teeth, peeked in on Julie and went downstairs.

I had several jars of tea brewing in the sun, and with the recent warmth, I was certain I could steal a bit and have a warm drink in the morning.

In the kitchen, I opened the cupboard for a mug and felt a breeze against my chest as it made its way through the slightly opened window. It didn't carry a stench. Either I was used to it, or the smell wasn't as bad.

Grabbing my mug I went out the back door to where I had the jars hidden just behind the dying plants on the patio. I supposed I didn't need to hide them, but I didn't want to take a chance of someone needing something to drink and stealing them.

The temperature reading was eighty. It was like an arctic blast compared to what we have had.

I fetched the jar placed by the blue flowerpot, twisted the lid and poured some in the cup. It felt and tasted good, I started to feel somewhat better. The baby kicked after the third drink, he liked it too.

As I sipped I noticed Bill fixing the pool covering. It struck me as odd because Millie told me they were leaving early.

Finally he spotted me and waved. I stepped from the patio nearer to him.

"Everything okay?" I asked. "I thought you guys were leaving."

"We were," Bill answered. "Then Millie wasn't feeling well. Her fibro was acting up and we decided to wait." He peered up to the sky. "Looks as if we caught a break in the weather. We'll know more when Larry gets back."

"Yeah, we will. I hope Millie feels better."

"When are you and the kids leaving?"

"Probably tomorrow," I said. "I'm waiting on Larry as well."

"If you hear anything before me, let me know," he said.

"I will. Give Millie my best," I told him then after grabbing a jar from the patio, I headed back to the house. When I walked in, Josh was in the kitchen.

He set a bag on the counter. "I brought some stuff. My mother said I needed my own rations," he said.

"They left?" I asked.

"Yeah, about two hours ago."

"Where are they going?"

"I have an aunt in Flagstaff, that's where they're headed. They said to go there, they'll leave word if they leave."

"Are you okay?" I asked.

"Yeah, I'm good. You? You look pale."

"The kidney stone is getting close to passing. It must be a big one." I was ready to explain how this was not my first round in the kidney stone rodeo when there was a knock on the front door.

Josh jolted and turned. "Stay here." He said with concern.

"Josh, really, it's fine," I said, heading from the kitchen. "Someone meaning us harm won't knock."

And I knew my words were correct when I saw Reverend Ray at the front door.

He looked tired. The usually, 'put together' crisp tee shirt and jeans, down to earth reverend was slightly disheveled. The handsome and youthful African American man was not his usual self at my door. In fact, in an off occurrence, he wore a baseball cap with a wrinkled Marvel Comics tee shirt and carried a clipboard.

"Morning, Tess. Sorry to bother you."

"Did you want to come in?" I asked, holding open the screen door.

"No, thank you."

With his decline to come in, I stepped out.

"Are you feeling all right?" he asked.

With his question, the third in twenty-four hours about my health, I decided to make a mental note to look in the mirror. I explained about my kidney stone and how it didn't go well with the pregnancy.

"Well, make sure you rest and get as much water as you can," he said. "I'm here to see if you need anything." He looked at his clipboard. "Sherriff has you listed as one of the people he took items from that didn't come to the distribution to get them back."

"You mean didn't loot."

"I was being polite about it."

"So basically, he listed me as one of the ones who didn't raid the center."

"Exactly."

"I'm okay, right now. Are there still items?"

"Yeah, they're at the church if you need some. I took over yesterday."

"Where's the sheriff?"

"He left this morning. That makes about half the town gone now."

"You're not going?" I asked.

"Unfortunately, I cannot," he replied. "We keep getting stragglers trying to go east and half of them coming through are pretty sick."

"What's wrong with them?" I asked.

"Flu like symptoms."

"What about Doc Stanley."

"He's doing what he can. He thinks it could be cholera. Then again, Dr. Melvin who is still in town thinks its radiation. I think ... it's the bird flu." He nodded to the carcass of a bird on the step. "Truth is no one knows. They're just sick. We set up the church and library as a makeshift clinic."

"What about the hospital."

"Three blocks is quite a walk when you have a church and distribution center to run as well."

"You know they aren't your responsibility," I said. "You don't have to take care of them."

"Yeah, I do, Tess," he said. "People are my responsibility. They need help. I'm here."

"Are they that bad? Will they get well?"

He shook his head. "They're that bad and whatever it is, and it seems to be contagious by close contact. No worries." He held up his hand. "I've been sanitizing and using precaution."

"I'm not worried. But I appreciate you stopping by."

"If you need anything you know where I am." He stepped back. "I'm gonna go check on Del and Mary right now." He pointed to next door.

"Oh, they left town. I think either yesterday morning or the day before. I haven't seen them. In fact

…" I walked down the step. "I put water in the door. Why don't you take it?"

"Are you sure? You don't need it?"

"We seem good right now and I plan on leaving tonight or tomorrow anyhow." I cut through the hedges and walked to Del's path. "I'll stop by before we do to say goodbye. Plus, I want to see what Larry has to say."

"Yes, I'm interested in that as well."

"So, might as well, take this water," I reached for the screen door. "I didn't count it in our rations …" I stopped, immediately and instantly I couldn't move and within seconds of grabbing that handle, the nausea I had been diligently fighting won the battle when a wave of stench blasted me the second I opened that door. I stumbled back, spun clockwise and without control vomit shot from my mouth. I tried to block it with my hand, but that small amount of tea I consumed seemed like a waterfall as it erupted over my fingers.

Ray rushed to me, extending a handkerchief. "Tess, are you …"

He stopped.

He didn't say anything. He caught the smell. "Oh my God," he said.

"Is that smell what I think it is?" I took the handkerchief, wiped my mouth and then my hands. I placed it in my pocket pretty sure he didn't want it back.

"It may be a pet or the birds. We can't be sure. You said they left."

Emotionally I responded, peering over my shoulder to him. "I didn't see them leave. Oh, God."

"I'll check." Ray cleared this throat, brought his hand over his mouth and stepped to the door.

I had to see, I had to know. Besides, I didn't think there was anything left in my stomach to throw up. Covering my mouth and nose with my hand, I followed Ray inside.

We didn't have to go far.

Both of them were right there and showing signs that they had been decomposing for days. The heat took their toll on them during life and after death.

Mary was in the chair, her head tilted to the side, eyes open and white. Her body was bloated in her housedress. Her legs, propped up on the recliner chair were so swollen the skin had split.

Del lay on the floor, he wasn't wearing a shirt, and he too was swollen. However his belly was distended and green, and it appeared to have burst. His insides, blackened, spilled out onto the living room carpet.

I had seen enough and I ran out.

Ray came out a few moments later, pulling the door closed.

"I covered them," he said. "Not that it matters. We don't have the hands to move them and bury them.

"Was it the heat?" I asked. "Lack of water?"

"I'd say both. The green stomach …" Another clearing of his throat. "That usually means the body reached an extremely high temperature."

My head dropped and I felt the sickening feeling in my gut, this one from emotions.

"Tess," Ray placed his hand on my shoulder. "There was nothing anyone could have done."

I nodded and didn't say anything. What could I say? I disagreed. There was something that could have been done. I could have offered help a little bit sooner. Maybe if I did, Del and Mary, a couple who were good to my family, wouldn't be rotting in their living room.

TWENTY – FROM THE LEFT

I couldn't wrap my head around it.

Del and Mary were gone. All I kept going back to was the fact that Del looked pale, told me Mary was ill and I did nothing. I had enough supplies in my house to help them, yet, I didn't want to part with those supplies until I knew I had enough for my family. Perhaps one unselfish act could have saved one of their lives. An act I failed to make. I would have to live with that the rest of my life.

No one came for their bodies. Undoubtedly Ray asked for help, but there were few left in town to deliver that help. In a day or so there would be even less. Ray tried his hardest to give comforting words after I confessed to him about what I had done.

"You can't blame yourself. You were watching out for your family."

Still. I had the choice. Ray proved that by his actions. He chose to stay in town when he could have left. I made a vow right there, if I had the choice again to help, to save someone's life by just being less selfish, I would.

Ray was summoned back to his church. More people had came in from the highway. I took it as a good sign. We still had time to leave town. Although we waited on Larry and to hear the news he would deliver.

Julie was simply devastated to learn about Del and Mary. My usually staunch and unaffected daughter was visibly shaken and slipped into another mode.

"The heat isn't good. When are we leaving?" she asked

"You think it's any better away from here?"

"Yes," She nodded. "If they are moving east into our town, they're leaving from something."

"We don't even know what it is," I said. "We can guess. But until then we will only be running from the unknown."

"Better than staying here and dying from it."

"If we are going to survive, we need to know what we're up against."

"I don't care." Julie folded her arms with defiance. "Statistically speaking, the longer we stay here, the more chance we have of dying of the heat. Look at you, Mom. You're pale."

"It's the kidney stone."

"How do you know it isn't the heat wreaking havoc on you?"

She was right. I didn't know.

"Why are you so adamant about staying and waiting?"

"I told you," I said. "We don't know what we're running from and we don't know what we're headed to."

"How about this?" Julie asked. "We do know what we're running from. The heat, the flames. What caused them, I don't care. We need to go."

She was right. It wasn't just me. It was her, Tag, Liam, Josh and the baby. "We'll go."

Julie exhaled loudly. "Thank you. When?"

"Even though it's cooler at night, it's dangerous. We'll leave in the morning, early."

"What about now?"

"Julie, we have a working SUV. One of the few. I can't take the chance that someone will find out. We may get attacked, overrun by people who are on foot."

"We can take people with us. It's big enough to fit a few more."

"Where do we draw the line? Who do we help? No. We go. Us and Sam. I'll talk to him." At that second there was a knock on the screen porch door. "Speak of the devil."

Sam was there. He didn't wait for me to answer, he stepped in. "I have news."

Excitedly, I made my way to him. "From Larry?"

"Well, he said he couldn't tell if the flames were moving. He said they didn't move much. But the flames are sucking in the oxygen, pushing bad air this way and before long, they'll need to feed and they'll be here in about four days, not to mention other things."

I cocked back. "Larry learned all that from going up today."

"No." Sam shook his head. "Larry looked at the fire. I learned all that from the radio." He smiled. "I made contact."

TWENTY-ONE – NOVA SCOTIA

The Mount Graham International Observatory in Arizona saw them coming about thirty minutes before they first arrived. Enough time to power down but not before sending out an emergency notification to anyone and everyone who needed to know. Government officials, FEMA, NASA. They even hit the prepper sites. A warning they believed fell upon deaf ears.

That was exactly how Sam started the conversation, my mind immediately thought alien invasion.

The observatory and a couple of observatories and centers were able to spare their electronics from the impending EMP, but they didn't think any of the big government places were so lucky. It took a few days but communication had rekindle and radio chatter was making its rounds.

Sam made contact. He was diligent about trying and I was grateful.

We went into Jeff's office so he could explain to me. I didn't want to scare the kids. I would explain to them once I knew what was going on.

Sam brought out a map of the world and drew a circle that encompassed the entire Pacific Ocean; the center of it seemed to be the Marshall Islands. North the edge of the circle extended to the Bering Sea, east across to the west coast of the United States and west, it went as far inland as Beijing. South it hit Australia.

"We were fortunate the Pacific took the brunt of it," Sam said. "This is based on the coordinates I got. This was the part of earth facing them. Everything in that circle was instantly and immediately obliterated."

116

"Them? What obliterated parts of the earth."

"Two," Sam said. "They call them the deadly twins. Gamma ray bursts. A long and short one. Happens when either two dead stars collide or a hypernova explodes. That's like a giant star. The short ones cause less damage, the big ones, well …" he whistled. "Like getting hit with all the power of the sun in one spot."

"Oh my God, you were right." I said.

"Now's not the time to brag. I wouldn't have guessed this. What I'm showing you is where it hit. The man I spoke to said they are communicating with satellites that are sending images. They expect the fires to stop close to Phoenix."

"So we need to get passed Phoenix?" I asked.

Sam shook his head. "There's a lot more, kid, a lot more. See, not only did these burst kill our electronics for most of the world, they punched a hole right in our ozone layer. We got not only fire, but the radiation that is seeping through."

"Is that what those people from the highway have? Radiation sickness?"

"I'm guessing so…"

"Is there radiation here now?" I asked.

"I checked. Nothing yet. But I assume it will be here in a few days."

"Then we need to get moving."

"We do," Sam said. "And far. That hole will spread. Eventually it will stop, be a giant open spot for the sun to just burn us out. In time, long after you and I are gone, it will close up. Hopefully. Until then, within two weeks, most of the United States and Asia, will be uninhabitable for a long time."

The news took me aback some, but I felt relieved to finally know what was going on. "What's the plan, then?" I asked. "What now?"

"They are telling people to go east. Go as far east and possibly north east as they can go."

"We'll never make it that far on what gas have."

"I have to tune in tonight again," Sam said. "Apparently, the warning was heard. There are convoys and trucks and trains taking people east. We go as far as we can and get as close as we can to one of those places picking up people and we're good. Who knows? We may be able to get gas somewhere. But there are problems out there."

"What do you mean?"

"We got to make sure we're not sick or we can't get on the transports. I know that much."

Hearing that made me chuckle in ridicule. "Really? They are scared of radiation sickness spreading or they just don't want to deal with the ill? Radiation sickness is not contagious."

"But other things are."

My attention caught. I crossed my arms and listened.

"Aside from some sort of virus from the dead birds. Dying people and animals are causing something else. Cholera. They have it. The birds have it. Animals. Without proper medical care, hygiene, it's an epidemic that we are ill equipped to handle."

I closed my eyes at the news.

"So we just need to get packed and go. Even though we have a few days. We shouldn't wait. First thing tomorrow. We're all well, none of us are sick, now's the time," he said.

I nodded my agreement. He had told me all I needed to hear. Of course there was more. If we successfully stayed well, made it through the borders, caught the transport and arrived to a safe zone, it wasn't over. The struggle to keep surviving would begin once we arrived east.

Throughout history extinction level events had occurred. I just never believed I'd be alive to see the day when the next one arrived.

It did and my family and I were not only witnesses to the end, we were also victims.

TWENTY-TWO – THE HAND

Doctor Stanley stopped by our street after hearing Sam had made contact. He needed more information about what he was medically dealing with. Supplies to help those who were ill were limited. There were many from the highway with radiation, less than a dozen with cholera and nearly twice that had some unknown illness.

We sat on my front porch, ignoring the smell. Yet, each whiff from the dead birds worried me. They weren't just bodies, they were carriers of something.

"I checked the medical books," Dr. Stanley said. "H5N1 isn't the only thing we can catch from dead birds. There's a laundry list. I can't treat what I don't know."

Sam understood, but there was nothing he could do until the people in Phoenix were back on the air at five p.m. He'd try.

Dr. Stanley was at his wits end.

"We have ten of our own townspeople down with it. How many more left this morning and are now getting sick? It has to be contagious."

"How long does it take to show symptoms?" I asked.

"Day or two from what I'm seeing."

There was something exceedingly frightening about hearing the word contagious. It meant, even if we were in the clear with radiation, we weren't with whatever else was going on.

"Is this why they're stopping people?" I asked. "I mean, cholera can be beaten."

"It can when caught early enough; this is definitely something respiratory. In the air or water. It's hard to tell. That is the thing I think the border patrols are worried about." He seemed so defeated. "Who knows. Just that, I'm sure those who came here sick weren't sick when they left their towns. Well, those without radiation poisoning. That is not a pretty sight."

Admittedly, I didn't understand what he meant by 'pretty sight' nor did I ask him to elaborate.

He waited a little while longer with me until Sam came from his house and said he was unable to make contact.

"It was worth a shot," Dr. Stanley said. "Find me when you do hear back at five."

"Will do, Doc," Sam said.

At that moment, we all lifted our heads to the green tinted sky when we heard Larry's plane.

Sam whistled. "Going east. Larry didn't waste much time now."

"Guess progress reports from Larry are done," I said.

Sam shrugged. "Do you blame him? Once he knew we could get information he felt free and clear to leave. He'll fly as far as he can."

"And hence … another leaves." Dr. Stanley stepped from the porch. "Pretty soon we'll all be walking across the desert to get out of here. Hopefully before the radiation catches us like the ones out west."

Both Sam and I remained silent as we watched him walk away. We both knew our journey east wouldn't be on foot, even in front of someone as kind as Dr. Stanley, we kept our ace close to our chest.

Not even he would know we had transportation. Although, he was a single man, a widower, so I was contemplating on asking him to join us. His knowledge and expertise would be vital.

"Sam?" I asked. "Why do you suppose the radiation hasn't reached here, yet?"

"I'm not an expert. Hell, I would have guessed it would be here by now. But air-flow, winds, the fire sucking in the oxygen, I guess they have a lot to do with it. It's creeping here though, that's for sure. Well …" He glanced down to his watch. "I better start getting things ready."

"Yeah, me, too." I bid my farewell for the moment to Sam, knowing I had so much to get ready. Julie was working on it. We had a lot of stuff. I wanted to not only get it into my SUV, but hide it somehow so we weren't a moving target.

My paranoia level increased by the hour. I knew how far I had gone, worrying obsessively, when I reached my door handle and heard a cough.

Turning my head to the sound I knew it came from next door; Bill's house. A manly cough, it was Bill. He coughed again.

Normally I wouldn't think anything of it, but after hearing the news about the new and contagious respiratory virus, that cough might as well have been an explosion.

It sounded frightening and had the potential to be deadly.

In my mind, a cough … a bomb … there was no difference.

The temperature stayed around eighty and was much more manageable inside. The increasing cloud coverage did have its benefits.

Julie rambled excitedly and fast about all that she had packed. About, how she found a map and a bag of weed in Jeff's special room. I felt exhausted, in pain, and not myself.

"Where's Josh?" I asked.

"He's helping Reverend Ray."

She must have noticed my concern because she held up her hands to stop me from speaking.

"Not with the sick. Going around looking for supplies and seeing if anyone needs anything."

"Well, adult or not, he needs to let me know. Since his parents left, I'm gonna take it they are trusting us to treat him like family…"

As soon as I said those words I froze and looked in the living room.

Liam sat on the couch holding a toy.

How easily I spewed forth those words about family in reference to a grown man, yet, I failed to see my responsibility to Liam, a child.

He had lost his family, he had no one. Yet, I treated him like a boarder or lost luggage, waiting for someone to claim. No one was going to claim Liam. Unconsciously, I ignored him, didn't even attempt to get close to him. Had I even spoke to him or paid attention to him in the last couple days?

Not only as a human being, but as a mother, I was failing. What was wrong with me? Had I been so consumed, I didn't even acknowledge the needs of a child.

Children needed three things, food, shelter and love.

Guilt consumed me; giving attention to him cost me nothing. It was something he wasn't getting. We were all he had. Instantly I felt horrible. I was a better person than I portrayed, at least I thought I was. The events of late had taught me I had a lot to learn as a human being.

I walked away in the middle of a conversation with Julie, went straight to the living room, sat on the couch and lifted Liam to my lap.

"I'm sorry," I whispered. "Can I hug you?"

He nodded and lifted the toy. "Like the truck?"

"Yes." I lifted him to my lap and secured my arms around him, trying my hardest to convey warmth and care. I noticed his cast. Obviously Tag had drawn all over it.

The child was injured, lost and alone and I did nothing.

That would change.

How long did I sit there holding him? Giving him my complete attention, even when Tag asked me for a story. I declined, telling Tag, 'Later' and dedicated my all to Liam at that moment. He needed and deserved it.

It was in the middle of hearing Liam's story, half of which contained words I couldn't make out, that Josh came in.

The look on his face told me he had something to say and was scared.

"What is it?"

He took a breath, moistened his lips, "There's people out on the highway, too sick to go any farther."

"Okay." I returned my attention to Liam.

"From what I hear it's radiation sickness. Nothing contagious."

"Okay." I said again.

"Can I take Julie and use your truck to go get them?"

I lifted my head. "No."

"There are five people …"

"No."

"Is that a no to taking Julie or …"

"To it all."

"They aren't contagious."

"I don't care. You can't take her, you can't take my truck. I need the gas and I don't want people to know about the truck. How do you know they aren't contagious?"

"The man that came in told us. They just need help."

I returned my attention to Liam.

"Tess, they'll die if we don't help them."

"They aren't our problem, Josh. They'll die anyhow …" As soon as I said those words, I cringed.

Did they just come from my mouth?

Me, the person who felt guilty about Liam. The same woman who not an hour earlier made a vow not to be selfish.

Yet, there I was, doing it again.

Slowly, I lifted Liam from my lap and stood. "You're not taking my daughter in case there's a problem."

Josh exhaled. "I can use the truck?"

"Yeah, I'll go with you."

"Tess, you don't look well. Maybe …"

"I'm fine. I'll go with you."

"Cool," he said. "I'll go put back the fuse." He walked toward the kitchen and the back door.

Julie stepped in the room. "Are you really going?"

"I am."

"Why?"

"Because I feel I need to and, not that I am a doctor or anything. But I'm gonna make sure these people don't have the virus before I bring them back to town."

"How will you tell?"

"Like I said, I'm not a doctor, but the doctor did say the radiation sickness wasn't a pretty sight. Something like that I think I'll be able to determine."

"Are you sure you want to go."

I nodded then said goodbye to the boys. I wanted to get outside and get moving before my motivation to perform an act of unselfishness left me. I suppose there would be those who wouldn't consider me selfish, that I was doing what I could for my family. But in the end, it wasn't for others to judge me it was for me to judge myself. Would I be able to look back and keep my head held high over things I did or didn't do?

The short trip through town was a heck of a lot different than it was a few days earlier. We only spotted a couple families making their way out of town on foot. Were they insane? Even though the temperature dropped, they wouldn't get too far before dark.

Everyone we passed looked at us driving by.

Before the EMP hit, SUV's rolling down the street were commonplace, now it was an anomaly.

It seemed everyone that had a working car had already left.

Storefronts were busted up. The streets were empty. And as we passed the church, it was the only place around with people. Reverend Ray had white canopy tents set up outside his church and people camped there.

Oddly, the only place in town with an abundance of life was also a haven for those facing death.

Josh told me the people weren't too far off the highway and that Reverend Ray mentioned the lone road straggler told about passing a wreck.

Liam's family, I guessed.

We had little conversation. My back ached and stomach twitched with nervousness. I informed Josh that if those on the highway looked as if they had the flu then we were turning back around. We couldn't take that chance.

He agreed.

We made it up the first hillside and just as we rounded that sharp bend, the small group came into focus and I stopped the truck.

There were duffle bags on the highway, a shopping cart that had suitcases in it. Four people lay on the road and one person, seemed to be a caretaker, a woman with a long ponytail. She was hunched down beside the person furthest from us.

On the outside chance it was a virus, Dr. Stanley had given Josh masks and we placed them on before stepping out of the truck. I couldn't see how the paper facemask would protect from any germs.

Despite the mask there was a sour stench that carried in the air. The first sick victim wasn't far from where we stopped. I caught one look at her and knew it wasn't a virus.

Dr. Stanley didn't exaggerate when he said it wasn't a pretty sight.

The woman lay on her side, a blanket covered her, and she shivered. Her hair was gone, body covered in purple bruises and open sores, and she attempted to sit up so as not to choke as she fought the violent retching.

Josh crouched down to her. "We'll get you some help."

He was lying.

There was no help to give. The best we could do was give her a ride to a more comfortable place to die.

"Help her in the truck," I said to Josh. "We have to figure out a way to get them all in. Maybe the caregiver is healthy enough to walk."

"I can walk with her, if there's not enough room."

"We may need to do that." I assessed those lying on the highway and focused on making my way to the caregiver.

Two steps toward her, my heart dropped to my stomach.

She turned around.

As soon as she saw me, her knees buckled and she nearly fell. She extended out her hand to me, calling. "Marmie."

It was Nicole.

Oh my God, Nicole. She made it all the way home.

I wanted to cry, scream, I was so overjoyed. My heart raced uncontrollably and my breathing went hyper as I hurried to her.

Nicole was alive.

The second I reached her, I grabbed hold and brought her to me, wrapping my arms as tightly around her as they would go.

"Oh my God," I held her so tight, I nearly crushed her. "You made it. You're alive."
"Oh, Marmie, I didn't think I'd ever see you again," she cried. "I'm so glad you're here. I'm so glad it's you that came."

I pulled back and ran my hand down her face. She looked tired but she didn't show any signs of sickness. "Me, too. And I'm so proud of you helping these people."

"Marmie, I had to," she said emotionally. "I couldn't leave him."

Just as I was about to ask, "Who?" I felt the touch to my ankle.

Someone had grabbed me.

I looked down. Fingers clutched tightly to me. The skin was burned some, but more so, open and blackened wounds covered the swollen hand.

My eyes followed the hand to the arm, and then I saw the face.

I saw the person lying on the ground. The one who grabbed hold of me.

It was the 'him' that Nicole couldn't leave.

It was her father, my husband…Jeff.

TWENTY-THREE - STALLED

There was a pain in my chest like no other I had ever felt. It was a physical pain, yet it wasn't. There was nothing physically wrong with me. A pain brought on by nothing more than sheer heartache.

I didn't know what was worse. Believing Jeff to be dead or seeing him like this on the side of the road.

I was grateful, beyond happy that Nicole was alive. She was in a woman's prison outside of San Bernardino; he was further south. How they came to be together I didn't know. I was certain I would find out. But my first mission was to get Jeff in the car.

"Oh, God, Tess, I'm a mess," he said but not with pity. Almost as if he were trying to make light of a dire situation. His tried to speak strongly, but I could hear it in his voice. The weakness. Something I never saw in my husband.

"Yeah, you are," I replied in the same manner. "But I've seen you worse."

"Oh, yeah, when?"

"Your brother's bachelor party."

He squinted his already swollen eyes. "I was pretty bad after that."

"Yes, you were."

Did Jeff know how bad he was? How horrible he looked? His thick mane was reduced to thin strands of baby fine hair. His scalp could be seen and it was covered with purple marks, black wounds. His lips were dry and cracked, the same sores were all over his body, along with blisters sporadically about his body.

He wore clothes, but seepage caused them to stick to him in spots.

When I tried to help him up, he lifted his hand, shook his head and turned from me to gag.

Nothing emerged. His body twisted and contracted as he fought to remove emptiness from his stomach.

When he was composed enough, he let me help him. But not much. I don't believe it was pride, I believe it was more pain when he was touched. Were they burns or just the effects of the heat and radiation?

Upon our arrival back at Falcon, Dr. Stanley would have the answers. At least I hoped.

While I tended to Jeff, I had Josh move the others to the car. One of them, a woman, had died before he could move her.

It was a strange situation. We didn't know what to do with her? Like with Liam's parents and siblings there was a sense of guilt just leaving her there. But there wasn't much we could do.

We were all able to get into my SUV. Jeff and the other two that were ill, sat in the back, barely able to sit up straight, leaning on each other. I had to put down the windows, the stench in the car was unbearable. It was sour and it was mixed with the odor of vomit and feces.

I held Nicole's hand the entire short trip back into town.

Once we arrived at the church, I instructed Josh to run back to my house, get Julie mentally prepared as well as sort out a place for Jeff to rest. I wasn't leaving him at the church.

Reverend Ray was probably exhausted and looked it when we arrived back with a couple more people.

"This was a good thing you did, Tess," he said. "The Lord…"

Then he saw Nicole. She was situating one of the new ill. Through his exasperation he smiled. "She was the caretaker on the highway?"

"Yes," I nodded. "Jeff is in the car. He's pretty bad. Can you send Dr. Stanley to my house when he returns?"

"Absolutely," he said. "I will stop by as well."

"Thank you." Though I wanted to stay and talk to Ray, find out what all I was to expect and needed to do for Jeff, I really had to go.

Had it not been for the woman's scream, more than likely from seeing Jeff in the back seat, I would never had known I was about to lose my car.

I turned around at the scream. My vehicle was parked maybe only ten feet away. But far enough that had it not been for Jeff in the car, Ben Collins would have been long gone with my only means out of town.

Back door open, he hurriedly tried to grab Jeff from the back seat and I rushed as fast as I could.

Shouting, "Leave him alone," I reached for his arm and he not only easily pulled his arm from my grip, he backhanded me hard across the face. The force of the hit sent me back and to the pavement but not before I saw Nicole rage forward.

Shoulder first she rammed into Ben, a man of average height. He bounced off the interior of the back door so hard I thought the door would fly off. Then Nicole plunged her fist into his gut with all she had. He reached out, grabbed her hair and prepared to hit her when she ended it.

From the back waistband of her shorts, she grabbed a revolver and fired one single shot, barrel against flesh, into his gut.

Ben's wife, Monica screamed as Ben slid down and to the ground.

Emotional, face stinging, and still on the ground, trying hard to get up, I saw that Nicole didn't bat an eye nor did she flinch in the aftermath of what she did.

She merely turned, flung open the driver's door and aimed inside. "You have three seconds to get out or I shoot. One ... two ..."

Monica screamed shrill.

"I *will* say three and I *will* shoot."

"Nicole!" Ray shouted. "Stop. Don't do this!"

She didn't look at Ray. "Three."

The passenger door flew open and I can only assume Monica jumped or fell out. I couldn't see.

Ray helped me to my feet. "You alright?" he asked me.

I nodded.

Nicole made her way over. "Let's go, Marmie. Let's go home." She grabbed hold of my arm.

"Nicole. Dear God," Ray had a scold to his voice. "Do you not care? You just shot Ben Collins. He was scared. You ..."

"Did what I needed to do," Nicole said. "My father is dying because someone like Ben was scared, took his car and my father had to walk in the radiation. Ben was not taking the only means to get my family to safety. Come on, Marmie."

Nicole moved fast to lead me to the car. I looked back at Ray. He was shocked and silent. Ben Collins wasn't dead, he was dying though...a huge pool of blood grew bigger by the second around him. His arms twitched, eyes stared blankly up as if searching the sky. Monica knelt in the river of blood, crying hysterically, looking at us as we pretty much stepped over them.

I glanced back once more at Ray and mustered up my best apologetic look. Truth was, I wasn't sorry. Not at all. I was glad that Nicole took control of the situation or else, like many others, we would have been walking out of Falcon's Way.

TWENTY-FOUR - HOME

Hearing Julie cry out a heart wrenching "Daddy," when she saw her father was spirit crushing. Not that I had much spirit left. The only thing that lifted it was seeing Tag race to his mother and seeing Nicole's expression when she held her son.

She agonized in getting home, she fought and she made it. Nicole wouldn't let him go. Their reunion was emotional and tear-filled, however it was almost overshadowed by the fact that Jeff was dying.

I had never seen a human being so sick in all my life. He had nothing physically left. My handsome husband was transformed into a shell of a being, a horror relic from some sort of movie. It wasn't real, I thought.

But it was.

He was the only one not suffering from the heat. I suppose that was a good thing. He shivered with fever and we had to keep him covered. He stayed downstairs in the family room. Even though it was only a few feet from the bathroom, there was no way Jeff could walk there.

Nicole told me he stopped eating, stopped taking water, because he couldn't keep anything in or down.

Tag didn't understand, nor would he ever, why his 'Pop-pop' looked so sick.

"Will he get better?" he asked.

I lied.

"Yes."

Julie, like me, was a seesaw of emotions. Joyful over having Nicole return and heartbroken over her father. Sam came over, took one look, shook his head and said, "I'm sorry."

He asked if we needed anything. I wanted him to take Tag from the house, just to get him away, but Nicole wouldn't let her son go.

I didn't blame her.

Jeff surprisingly kept fighting. To speak with him and hear him talk, I wouldn't know he was so sick. But looking at him, there was no way he wasn't knocking on death's door.

I prayed for a miracle.

But had I already received one? I had written both him and Nicole on the death list yet there they were ... home.

How?

"Daddy came for me," Nicole said. "He came for me."

Hearing this not only shocked me but made me cry. Jeff disowned her, he made no bones about it. Hardcore about disowning Nicole ...but he went for her.

"When I got to the school, it was only a few minutes before the first EMP hit," Jeff said. "The word was out on campus. It was just an EMP. My car was off. I took out the battery. We were pretty sure it would run. But I couldn't leave. I stayed below until the next one hit."

"You were a hundred miles from Nicole."

"I was fool," Jeff said. "I should never have let it go on." his voice cracked. "She is my child. And when that second one hit, I thought of her. I knew you guys would be okay, but she was there, at that prison. If it was the last thing I did, I would get to her. I couldn't live my life without letting her know I loved her. Too much time was lost."

Nicole had returned into the room in the middle of Jeff telling me. But he grew weak and went to sleep. She told me when the burst hit, the locks released, but they were still on the prison grounds.

"My first thought was to get home, to get to Tag," she said. "But we didn't know what was going on. So we waited, thinking we'd hear something. Then the birds started dropping from the sky and people started getting sick. Real sick, real fast. Anyone out in the yard when the birds fell got sick. I felt bad leaving. Then two days ago, Daddy showed up. He had walked."

"Your father walked a hundred miles."

"He got a ride the last bit. But someone stole his car and he started walking. He didn't know that his area was full of radiation. He was so sick when he arrived, Marmie."

"How did you get this far?"

"We packed in cars, then about thirty miles ago we had to walk. He was too weak to continue. So I stayed and sent someone into town. He came for me," she lowered her head. "I thought my father hated me but he came for me. I could never leave him."

It was emotional. Jeff, who swore up and down he didn't have a daughter named Nicole, who wrote off his very own flesh and blood, had put his life on the line to see her one more time.

Nicole stated over and over she couldn't leave him.

How was I to tell her, we had to move again? That we had to leave and wherever we were going Jeff could only go so far.

Then again, I didn't think Jeff would survive much longer.

He was bad. He was really bad.

He did however ask for his stash. I gladly helped him enjoy some of that weed he had hidden in the basement. I knew it would give him some relief from what he was experiencing.

Dr. Stanley stopped by and told us he was in the late stages. A day or two and Jeff would leave us.

While grateful Nicole was fine and with us, I couldn't bear the thought of losing Jeff. Despite the fact that I accepted it beforehand, it wasn't a reality. Now it was and I had to face it.

Once the day had calmed, and a quiet set in, I started feeling poorly again. Perhaps it was the heat, maybe I needed to pop in at Sam's, even just for a few minutes.

Even though it was nightfall, there was a strong buzz of flies. I could hear them even in the house.

I told the girls I would return, and I stepped out on the porch. It was dark, the moon was buried beneath the haze, but out front was a light.

The night before that same lantern was there as Bill buried his dog.

Now Bill was out there again, digging another hole.

My throat swelled up and my face felt tense. I hated to ask because I knew. I just knew.

"Bill?" I spoke softly.

"Hey, Tess." He sniffed and wiped the back of his hand under his nose. "Sorry about Jeff. I saw you guys pull up."

"Thank you." I nodded. "What's ... what's going on?"

"I lost my Millie. She passed away a couple hours ago."

"Oh, Bill, I am so sorry."

138

"Yeah," He said, shoved the shovel in the ground and coughed. "Keep your distance, Tess, I think I may have it too."

"Not everyone gets it. Nicole was around it and she's fine. Maybe it's just the smoke."

"Maybe."

"I'm really sorry, Bill, I am."

"So am I."

Not really knowing what else to say to him, I was glad to see Sam standing out on his porch. I wished Bill well then made my way over to Sam's.

"Tess, you look paler."

"I'm worn out," I said.

"You're sick.'

"Not with any flu," I said. "It's just emotional, this weather, the pregnancy and now this kidney stone will not pass."

"I got extra water, maybe you should drink some more."

"Maybe."

"How's Jeff?"

I sighed out and hung my head. "Oh, Sam, he's bad. He's so bad. And it breaks my heart. He's a good man."

"You're family is together, that's a positive thing." Sam said. "We're supposed to head out tomorrow."

"I know. But we also know, no matter where we get to, they won't let Jeff through."

"Yeah, we do." Sadly, Sam nodded.

"And we'll probably run out of gas before that anyhow. He won't be able to make the walk." I paused. "What should I do, Sam? I can't leave him. I can't take him. He doesn't deserve to die out on the side of the road. He doesn't. But…"

"Stop." Sam held up his hand. "They're saying we have three days. We'll see that fire over the ridge. Hell we'll feel it. We can wait."

"But the kids…"

"We'll get then kids to safety in plenty of time."

"You don't have to stay," I said. "You can go."

"Nah. You guys are all I have. I'm not leaving you. You're stuck with this grumpy old man."

At that I just grabbed him and hugged him. Poor Sam didn't know what hit him. He certainly didn't expect it. I needed to. After a moment, he finally responded and returned the embrace. It felt good. I was a woman on the brink of breaking, physically and mentally. I had reached my end and I just needed something, someone to hold on to. Sam was it.

I was so emotional I couldn't speak. If I could, at that moment I would tell him, grumpy old man or not, I wouldn't want it any other way.

Somehow though, even if I didn't say it, Sam knew I felt that way.

TWENTY-FIVE – THIS STONE WILL PASS

July 14

I found myself sitting there, staring at Jeff. Watching him breathe. Watching him struggle. His chest rising and falling at a slow pace. I did so for the longest time after everyone was asleep. Until Jeff opened his eyes, looked at me, and said, "I'm not dead. Yet."

He smiled. For the last several years I have fought, struggled, to remember why I married him. It took until he was so close to death. So close to me losing him, for me to realize. It was that quirky sense of humor that had me from the starting gate. The one that came out at the oddest times was the number one reason I fell in love with him.

I started to think back and reflect on when we first met. How I was absolutely miserable working at the quick mart back in Los Angeles. He came in for chewing tobacco and there was a minor earthquake. As corny as it sounded, he made me laugh when he said, "That's a sign you should go out with me. See? We can move mountains."

Then he started singing Carole King's, *It's too Late*. Of course, I had no idea what that was.

That was our beginning. In a crappy convenience store the day of a four point one.

Now here was our end.

In a beautiful home on a Father Knows Best Street a few days after the earth was scorched.

Ironically we started and ended with jolt from nature.

Though, according to Jeff, he wasn't dead yet. There was still a chance of a miracle. I prayed for one. I would give anything for one more chance with Jeff, for him to get well.

I told him I was sorry more than once, I wanted badly for the chance to show him how sorry I was for the last few years.

I was happy. I just didn't realize it.

I did love him when I didn't show it.

At the end his breathing labored, but he was fighting. The late night into early morning was spent between sitting with Jeff, going up to check on Tag, then back down the stairs.

Just as the sky lightened enough for me to look at the clock and realize I had been up all night, I made up my mind to get some rest. I had been in that chair next to Jeff all night.

The house was quiet and I noticed there was a different tint to the outside. Previously it had been greenish, but now it looked orange.

Worried, hands bracing the arms of the chair, I stood and that was when it hit me.

The achy and sharp discomfort from the kidney stone felt like a burning knife in my back. The sensation shot through my abdomen, radiated down my groin and to my thighs. As soon as I stood, my legs weakened and a ripping pain struck between my legs and it felt as if my vagina was being torn from my body.

As if I weren't already overheated, I was thrown into a sweating frenzy and my stomach knotted and twitched. The room spun around me and I was in so much agony, I wanted to scream. In fact, I tried. But the pain was so intense it inhibited me from making a sound.

Help.

I needed help.

There was no way I was making it up the stairs and even trying to call for someone to help me was impossible. My faculties began to leave me and I wasn't thinking clearly.

I staggered my way from the family room to the front door, holding on to what I could to stay upright.

My name was called, but it was hard to tell who was speaking it. It was slow and distorted, muffled as if put through some sort of voice distorter.

"Tess … Tess ... you all right?"

Did I shake my head?

I tried to answer, but I couldn't and I pushed open the screen door. Maybe I needed air.

The second I stepped outside, everything spun and blurred. I grasped the porch railing with two hands, descended the two steps and as another unbearable pain blasted me, I caught through my peripheral vision, the two graves in Bill's yard.

My God, they'll be digging one for me, I thought.

I was next. Surely, with this much pain, I was dying.

Across my yard, barely keeping on the path, I wrapped my arms as much as I could around my stomach and moved in a zigzag fashion.

Where was I going? What did I hope to find?

"Tess." My name was called again.

Then I saw Sam open his screen door. It gave me a sense of salvation.

Sam, help me, please help me, I begged in my mind. *Please.*

He saw me, and he raced out.

Then along with the pain, I felt an enormous sense of pressure just before I felt something 'pop', and with that came wetness, a lot of it, running between my legs.

No. My legs buckled and I dropped to the yard, landing on my knees. Fearful, I reached down to my thighs and to the dampness.

Had my water broke?

I felt the warmth there and then lifted my hand to eye level just as Josh and Sam both arrived at my side.

My fingers trembled. I was crushed when I saw what covered my hand. It wasn't amniotic fluid or urine. It was blood, so much blood.

Suddenly upon seeing the blood, came the horrific realization that I wasn't passing a kidney stone, after all.

TWENTY-SIX - EMPTY

It was over and I knew it. I wanted to just stay put, but Josh swept me up into his arms and took off running with me. He carried me the entire way to the church where he knew Dr. Stanley had set up camp.

Sam was with us.

Both of them kept giving me words of encouragement.

Hold on, Tess, We're getting you help.

Was there help to give?

My body bounced in Josh's arms as he ran with me. Each bounce sent more pain through me and then the worst hit me. It not only grabbed me physically but tore at my soul when I felt the need to bare down.

I was still in Josh's hold.

Again, everything was still a blur, and I could only hear their voices.

"She's bleeding," Josh said. "Pretty bad."

"She's been sick for days," Sam said. "Said it was a kidney stone."

"Set her down here," Dr. Stanley instructed.

The moment, Josh laid me down on a cot I felt another contraction and fought the urge to push.

Dr. Stanley laid his hands on my stomach. "This isn't a kidney stone."

"It's too early for the baby, right?" Josh asked. "She's only like six months."

I saw the look on Dr. Stanley's face. He simply said, "Yeah," then looked at me. "Tess. Tess, listen to me."

"The blood. Why is there so much blood?" I asked breathy.

"The heat, the lack of water, the stress…" Dr. Stanley leaned close. "This isn't gonna be good, okay? I need you to work with me."

At that moment Ray came over. "Is there anything I can do?"

Dr. Stanley nodded. "Find Janice. We need to get her blood. Tess, do you know your blood type?"

"A," I answered.

"I'm A," said Sam. "You can take my blood for her."

"That will work, go with Ray," Dr. Stanley returned his attention to me.

I was certain more was going on than I was able to comprehend, but I was overwhelmed with the phase of bearing down. My eyes drifted to the roof of the tent. Voices meshed around me.

It wasn't happening. Yet, I knew it was. I transitioned from being in excruciating pain to the point of feeling an end. Relief was near.

Josh grabbed onto my hand, while Dr. Stanley finished rapidly undressing me. No sooner were my shorts off my body, I ejected into a sitting position and was no longer able to contain the desire to push. Nature took over. It was out of my control.

I believe it was only two pushes, and the sounds of my own cries, my own heavy breathing along with Dr. Stanley and Josh's words of encouragement became nothing more than ear deafening silence the second my child was born.

No one said a word.

I closed my eyes tightly, rested back, bringing my arm over my eyes.

"I'm sorry, Tess." Dr. Stanley said. "I'm so sorry."

I couldn't look. I didn't want to look. I truly believed at that second, if I didn't open my eyes it wasn't real.

It was real. It was painfully real.

Never in my wildest imagination did I think for a single second that I wouldn't give birth to a healthy child. A lot of things about my unborn baby crossed my mind not one of them were me losing him.

I was not mentally prepared for it. Yet, I had to face it.

Josh covered me and Dr. Stanley approached my side holding a towel wrapped bundle.

"I can take him away…"

"No." I whimpered. "No. I need to see him. I need to hold him."

With Josh's help, I sat up and Dr. Stanley extended the tiny bundle to me.

My heart broke as I tried to cradle him in my arms. He was fragile and weighed barely anything. His eyes were closed as was his mouth. He had a peaceful look on his face that was smaller than a baseball. His hands were inconceivably small.

Despite how beautiful he was, he was missing one thing … life.

He never got to take his first breath. He was robbed of that.

I would never get to hear him cry or laugh. The only thing I could do, the only thing I had was the chance to hold him.

And I did.

Dr. Stanley said that there was nothing that could be done. That my son, had passed away in the womb at least a day or so ago and my body was just expelling it. Expel. It sounded so harsh, and when Dr. Stanley said it, it showed on his face that perhaps it wasn't the right word choice.

It was harsh. But nothing *wasn't* harsh about what had happened.

The warning signs were all there. But I didn't see them or somehow refused to believe them.

One moment I thought I was fighting a kidney stone when in actuality I was fighting to keep my child inside of me.

I lost.

He lost.

Despite what Dr. Stanley said, my son, didn't die a few days earlier. I felt him kick. I know I did. Or did I?

Having a stillbirth was no different than a live birth … physically that is. Emotionally it is a whole other ball game. There was no pain with a gain, no exhilarated feeling of happiness that made the pain seem to disappear. The only thing emotionally that was the same was the overwhelming instant love. A love that brought heartache.

I still had to deliver the afterbirth. At least I stopped bleeding so badly.

It was still morning, I had received that blood transfusion and rested, and then after Reverend Ray gave me some clothes from the church bizarre, I headed home. Sam ran to the hospital and found a wheelchair. Sitting in it, I felt pathetic. I wanted to cry, just curl up in a ball and break down. But I couldn't. I had to be strong, keep going.

Once again, I asked Josh to run to my house, to let everyone know what was happening. That poor boy was the messenger of bad news. I was very grateful to him and Sam for being there.

"Are you, okay, kid?" Sam asked. "I mean, physically." He rolled me down the road. I carried my lifeless child in my arms. I hadn't named him; I wanted to do that with Jeff.

Poor Jeff, he wanted this baby so badly, promising that this time around he was going to do it all, that he wanted to do it all and I could enjoy life and not be bogged down with diapers and midnight feedings. I wanted to believe him, but I knew Jeff. It was a nice gesture though.

"I feel better," I said. "Physically."

Sam stopped rolling me. He brought his mouth close to my ear and whispered. "I so sorry Tess for what you are going through. I am." He kissed the top of my head and moved on.

We ventured the rest of the short distance in sad silence.

When we arrived back at my home, Jeff was out on the porch. Again, his dismal appearance took me aback. He stumbled to stand, and tried, he really did, to walk to me. But he was too weak.

Sam brought me to the edge of the porch where Jeff stood holding on to the post.

Nicole came flying from the house, as did Julie.

I hated the way they looked at me. Full of sadness and pity, my heart was already broken.

Slowly I stood from the wheelchair and walked up the few steps to Jeff.

He whimpered when he saw me with the bundled and covered baby.

"I'm sorry, Jeff," My voice cracked.

I stood directly in front of him and he took the baby, softly breaking down as he did. He didn't unravel the blanket to see, he just brought the baby to his chest and then reached out for me.

Nicole reached out for me. Julie reached out.

"Marmie, we're sorry." Nicole said kissing me on the cheek.

As I stood in Jeff's weak embrace, Julie embraced me from behind. "I love you, Marmie. I'm so proud of you for being so strong."

I closed my eyes tight to hold in the tears. Before walking back in the house, she leaned down and kissed the bundled baby.

"I'll leave you two to have your privacy," Sam said.

Jeff stepped back and looked around me. "Thank you, Sam, for being here for my family."

"I love them. I'm not going anywhere." He placed his hand on my back. "Take care of yourself, Tess. See you in a little bit."

Jeff looked at me. "I'm not gonna say the word sorry, that's a given, I wish I could have been there for you."

"I know."

He peered down to the baby. "We wanted to call him Russell. We need to give him a name before we bury him."

"Russell it is."

"Hey, Russell," Jeff said softly. "I know you hear me somewhere. I don't want you to be scared, ok, or lonely, cause I'll see you soon."

"Jeff…"

"No, Tess, I will," He passed on a tight-lipped smile then looked back down to the baby. "I'll hold you for your mom, I'll be there. I promised her before you were born that I had it covered." He looked back up at me. "I guess I will."

"My heart is broken Jeff."

"Mine, too." He leaned forward and kissed me on the cheek. "You'll get through this, Tess. It's gonna be a long road, but I'll tell you what, there couldn't be a better person than you to lead my family into tomorrow."

I held on to my weakened husband, knowing it was taking everything he had to be strong at that second. To stand up, hold our son and me.

We stayed on the porch only for a little while until Reverend Ray returned.

Just like the day before when Bill buried his wife, we buried Russell in the front yard.

It was a horrible day, one I would not soon forget. The only saving grace was there wasn't time to mourn, to feel self pity, there wasn't time for that at all. We just had to go on.

TWENTY-SEVEN – BOURBON

I was pretty useless the rest of the day. There wasn't much physically I could do. I wasn't in pain, but I was weak and when I moved too much, I would bleed. I had to remember I had a day or two before that let up.

There was nothing about me that felt whole. I was hollow, emotionally and physically. But there was so much to do, to get ready. It seemed cruel and sad that our departure hinged on when Jeff would die.

Tag hung out with me, but seemed scared of Jeff. I couldn't blame him. Liam on the other hand didn't know Jeff before he was sick and actually pestered him quite a bit. Jeff didn't look to be left alone.

"Bother me," he said. "Surround me with life. It's the last I will see."

By mid afternoon, the outside temperature was only ninety. Though that sounded high, it wasn't in comparison to what it had been. We moved to sitting outside. Watching the sky. There was an orange hue to everything and it wasn't bright. The sky west had a hint of pink. I also saw a steady stream of smoke. At first I worried it was the fire, but then common sense kicked in and I realized it was burning bodies.

"It's been like that since I can remember," Jeff said. "Worse when I was searching for Nicole. Hot as hell."

"It was hot here."

"No, I mean, unable to breathe hot. The only reason I made it through that heat was I kept breaking into any business I could find and dousing myself with water constantly, I think at one point it hit one-twenty."

I listened to Jeff talk, he had his wits about him, and it was hard to imagine he was so sick. A part of me truly thought he might get better.

Although Jeff indulged in a steady ritual of pot smoking. I didn't say a word. It made him feel better. Me, there wasn't much that would make me feel emotionally better. It had been months since I had an adult beverage and I broke out that bottle of bourbon. I had made up my mind to slowly nurse that bottle. Even though alcohol caused dehydration, I didn't care. I needed to feel numb.

We were out there a little while, and just before supper Bill came over for the wheelchair. Said, "Sorry about the baby' then asked if we were gonna use it and when I said no, he took it. A few moments later he was placing belongings in it.

"Are you leaving?" I asked.

"Yeah, gonna walk when the sun is low," He coughed. "Hopefully, someone will see me and get me. Give me a ride if I'm lucky. If not you'll probably see me on the side of the road somewhere. I have plenty of water. There's supposed to be several refugee stops between here and Glendale. Steady trucks helping move folks. That's what I heard."

"They aren't letting sick people on the transport."

"Not what I heard. Well, some transports are taking the sick. Maybe…you need to head out," he said with a nod to Jeff.

Jeff softly laughed. "I'm gonna die on the highway. Or in some refugee camp. If I am still hanging on when they need to go, then they go."

Bill grumbled. "You should go. And…" he then looked at me. "I'm not sick. This cough is part of some sort of bacterial infection. Millie said that's what she had. Thinks we got it from the pool, the dog too. I wasn't in there as long as they were. Neither was Tag, that's why he's not sick."

I had to admit I did panic a moment about Tag and that pool, but he wasn't sick. But I didn't believe for one second Bill didn't have that flu.

"Did Sam tell you about the refugee camps?" I asked. "He didn't mention anything to me about them taking the sick."

"I'm not sick," he repeated then coughed. "No, I heard it myself. Been picking up transmissions on the old transistor since yesterday morning. It's just a steady message, a repeated recording, but it's something to go by." He looked up to the sky. "I wouldn't stay here much longer. They said those in the Palm Springs area should be gone before the eighteenth."

"That's four days. We'll be gone."

"That's four days until the flames get here. I'm guessing the day before it won't be habitable with the heat. So make sure you go."

"We will."

Bill bid his farewell and we wished him well on his journey. He was walking in the heat and he was over sixty. I truly hoped someone helped him and gave him a ride.

I thought about what he said and turned to Jeff. "Did you want to try and go?"

"And die running?" Jeff asked. "Nah..." He reached over and grabbed my hand. "But that should not stop you from going."

"It's not. We have plenty of gas. Josh siphoned a lot. We got enough to get us close to Phoenix for a transport. We may have to walk some, but we have time."

"I won't make walking...some. Heck, I won't make walking at all." He paused. "Tess, you think maybe there's some truth in what Bill said. Maybe he has a bacterial infection after all."

Before I could answer, I heard Dr. Stanley reply. "No. Bill has the flu. Millie had that flu. Sadly." Dr. Stanley looked up the road to Bill who was moving along. "He'll be gone in about a day and a half. If he's not...then it's not the flu."

"Hell of a way to determine a diagnosis," I said.

Dr. Stanley shrugged. "The best I can do. How are you two?"

"I'm okay," I answered.

"Jeff?"

"Swell."

"Hmm. Are you eating? Drinking?"

Jeff shook his head. "Not always. I don't want them to waste water or food on me. I can't keep it in."

Dr. Stanley tilted his head. "If you didn't look so bad, I'd wonder how sick you actually were."

"It's the weed talking," Jeff said. "I'm stoned. I'll have some water in a bit, that's when I keep it down. What brings you by Doc?"

"I was able to find a car and it worked. Josh was very helpful in getting me gas," he said. "I'll be leaving."

"When?" I asked.

"Not tomorrow, but first thing the next day. I want to catch a transport."

"Reverend Ray?" I questioned. "Is he leaving too?"

"No. He's staying, unless everyone passes, he will stay. Eight more sick refugees just got into town. I admire him for doing this. It's noble. But I'm not noble."

"You're a lot nobler than you think you are," I said. "You've stayed this long."

He nodded once sadly. "Well, I'll leave you be. I'll check back on you tomorrow sometime. Just wanted to give you the heads up." After turning and stepping from the porch, he stopped. "Tess, I know you want to stay behind with Jeff. But you have children that need to live. You need to think about leaving here when I do."

I didn't respond to that. How could I? Jeff was right there and a part of me thought it was cruel to say anything but goodbye to the doctor.

Once he was gone, Jeff grabbed my hand. "He's right. You and the kids need to leave."

"We will. When the time is right."

"When will the right time be?" he asked. "When I die?"

I lifted my glass of bourbon, took a sip and stared blankly. I didn't reply.

TWENTY-EIGHT – CHANGING

Once the high wore off, Jeff fell asleep. It didn't last long. The reality that he was ill was evident once he wasn't stoned. Any water or the broth he ate came right up. He struggled with gagging and vomiting for an hour.

It was in that time he started scratching and with each scrape of his nails against his arm, he pulled skin.

I wanted to cry.

It was horrible what he was going through. He was suffering.

I felt somewhat stronger and was moving around more. The girls and Josh had packed everything they could in the car. Falcon's Way was a ghost town. There wasn't a sound or soul left, at least not that we could see.

Sam came to see me and I was comfortably numb from my consumption of bourbon.

I was pretty much convinced that Jeff wasn't making it through the night and I was trying to come to terms with that.

"How you holding up?" Sam asked as we sat on the porch.

"Better, at least the temperature tonight is tolerable. I'm not in pain."

"Physically," He said.

"Physically, you're right. Sam..." I faced him. "Listen, I am so sorry that you have to wait on us. Please know, I won't put you in danger. We will leave in time for the transports."

"I know."

"Are you listing them?"

157

"I am. They don't change. I did check, I couldn't find that recording that Bill mentioned to you."

"He was pretty adamant it was there."

"I'll find it."

"I just can't make Jeff leave, not now."

"Why are you justifying this to me?" he asked.

"Because you're waiting on us. We're your ride out of here."

Sam chuckled. "You think? I have a car. Gas too, thanks to Josh."

"Oh my God, what is Josh, the gas guy?"

"Considering he has nothing else to do, then yes."

"Why haven't you left?"

"No need to take two cars. We can fit in yours. And why leave alone? Nah, Tess, I'll leave with you guys. That little guy, he's been my lifeline since my wife died. Every day Tag made me smile. I'm not leaving that or your girls. I'll wait. Besides, you guys need me with you."

"We do."

"See this old man is good for something."

"You've been a godsend."

At that moment, the screen porch door squeaked open and Tag stepped out.

"Marmie?"

"Hey, baby, you're not sleeping?"

He shook his head. "I want to go to bed with you."

"Okay, where's your mom?"

"She's sleeping."

"I'll be right in."

"Will you tell me a story?" he asked.

"I will."

And then Tag stood there. He didn't go back in the house.

"I'll take that look," Sam said as he stood. "As my hint to leave."

"You don't have to go."

"It's late, the little guy needs you and I want to be on the airwaves to catch the next update."

"I take it the generator is running fine."

"Oh, yeah, lots of gas thanks to Josh." Sam leaned down and kissed me on the forehead. "I'll check back in the morning. Try to get some rest. You had a rough day."

"I will."

After Sam had left, I stood slowly from my porch chair and held my hand out to Tag.

"Help your Marmie up the stairs."

He gripped my hand. "I will."

"You're such a big guy," I said. 'Thank you for hanging out with me tonight."

"I'm used to sleeping in your bed."

"Can I tell you a secret?" I paused. "I'm used to you being there too."

Tag was my lifeline.

The greatest little guy in the world, he stayed by me as I slowly took the stairs. When I got to my room, I opened the windows. The temperature had dropped. It was going to be a tolerable night.

He lay on the bed, on his side, waiting on me and I slipped next to him. He peered up to me with his big eyes.

"Tell me a story, Marmie."

"What kind of story?"

"Something fun. Maybe …Tag against the dinosaurs."

I smiled.

I took tales of the past and substituted Tag in the story as a hero. Tag and The Three Bears. The Three Little Pigs and Tag. Then if he wanted something specific, I searched my movie database and substituted him there. I wasn't original, but he didn't know that.

Never did I get to the end of a story, he always fell asleep.

"Once upon a time. There were these scientists. They wanted to bring back dinosaurs, I said. "And they created them in a lab."

"Are there real scientists?" he asked.

"Of course."

"Are they smart?"

"Very."

"Can they make dinosaurs?"

"Probably."

"Marmie, if they can make dinosaurs, why can't they make everything better."

"They probably can, sweetie," I said. "We're just kind of in the dark here at Falcon's Way."

"Marmie? Is it the end of the world?"

I hesitated in answering. "Tag, where did that come from?"

"I'm pretty smart. I hear you guys talk. Is it?'

"No. No it isn't. It's just like a test. Like you get in school. Only we are being tested to see if we survive."

"Will we pass?" he asked.

"Yes, Tag, we will." I pulled him closer to tell the story and that was when I noticed.

My heart sunk and I prayed it was the weather and my imagination.

I hoped it was, because at that moment, Tag felt warm, he felt very warm.

TWENTY-NINE - TAG, YOU'RE IT

July 15

When I was child, our family had a collie named, Julius. I never knew a time in my life when Julius wasn't around. I didn't quite understand my parents always telling me he was old. Then again, as I hit my teens, I started to see it.

His moves were less agile, bark was deeper and strained, but he never left my side. My mother told me he was my personal watchdog since we got him.

He lived a lot longer than most dogs. He died just before my seventeenth birthday and I vowed because of the pain that I would never have another dog.

That night, after losing the baby, after just hitting my emotional end, I dreamt of Julius.

If I was late for school or was still sleeping after my parents were up and gone, Julius would bark. Jump on me and bark.

For a moment there, I was lucid in my dream. Knowing it was a dream and even justifying why I was dreaming about Julius. Things were rough, I had losses, and Julius was a painful reminder of those loses.

He kept barking.

Finally, I was so lucid that I woke up and realized it wasn't Julius barking, it was Tag.

Lying next to me, sound asleep on his side, Tag coughed.

He was oblivious to it. His little body jolted with each violent and deep cough.

"Oh my God," I reached over and touched him.

Hot.

His skin was so hot to touch it was frightening.

Immediately I jumped from bed. Something I shouldn't have done. I grew dizzy, so dizzy. I thought I was going to pass out.

"Nicole!" I called out. "Nicole!"

Holding on to the bed, I looked at Tag. He didn't stir. Once more I called out, "Nicole." Then made my way over to Tag's side of the bed. "Baby." I shook him gently. "Baby, wake up. Oh my God."

I brought my lips to him, hoping my hands were feeling wrong. But the sensitivity of my lips told me his fever was high.

Lifting the bottle of water from the nightstand, I grabbed part of the over sheet on the bed, doused it with water, and slowly wiped him down.

Not him.

It would be my last straw.

If something happened to Tag, I was done.

Nicole raced into the room and saw me next to her son.

"Marmie?"

"He's sick," I said barely able to breathe. "Send Josh, someone run and get Doc Stanley."

Instead of following my instruction, she hurried to the bed, placed her hand on him. I knew as a mother myself, I would do the same, hoping and wishing it wasn't true.

Nicole whimpered when she touched him.

"Go." I told her. "I can't leave. Just go."

After quickly kissing Tag, she raced from the room.

◇◇◇◇

Dr. Stanley wore protective garb. A mask, gloves, hood. Just like one of those doctors you would see in some sort of science fiction virus movie. Reverend Ray, on the other hand stated he put his faith in God and washed his hands.

After a quick examination of Tag, Dr. Stanley looked at us as if we were all doomed.

"None of you should be too close," he said outside the bedroom door. "In fact, I'd go as far as to say Tess, you shouldn't go anywhere. Not yet."

I honestly didn't plan on it.

"The rest of you need to stay away from the room or cover up if you go in. He has … Tag, I'm sorry, has the flu that's been going around."

"How can you be sure?" I asked.

"His fever is already dangerously high. He's not responding. I'm sorry Tess."

Standing next to Nicole, I watched as she lowered her head.

"The only positive thing about this sickness is it's fast," Dr. Stanley said. "Day and a half, two days tops."

"Bill said his wife and he both got some sort of bacterial infection," I said. "From the pool. Maybe Tag…"

'This isn't a bacterial infection, Tess."

Nicole asked. "How do you know?"

"I don't. But…time is the only thing that will tell. Unfortunately, right here in Falcon's Way, we don't have the luxury of waiting. I'm sorry."

He wasn't as sorry as we were.

Julie whimpered and cried, as did Nicole.

Jeff was lucky; he had slipped into a deep sleep and was out of it. I envied how he didn't have to feel the pain.

First him, then the baby…now Tag?

Dr. Stanley was sorry? Basically he was telling us we had two days.

I had two days left with my grandson. The child I spent every single moment of the day with, the child that took over Jeff's spot in bed and never left my side.

Two days?

If that was all I had left, then I wasn't missing a single second of it. I left Dr. Stanley in the hallway and returned to Tag's side.

THIRTY – ACCEPTANCE AND DECISIONS

Never in my entire life had I doubted the existence of God, maybe because there was never a need to. I hadn't faced anything so traumatic that I found myself saying, "Why, God?" My life was normal, uneventful. My childhood was good. My parents didn't abuse me. I had good friends, and had the average life. Like many I went to college for something inane that never was going to be a career. The loss of my parents was a huge impact, but I put my faith in God, as I did when Nicole's mother died. To me there was a reason that all three of them went so fast and unexpected. God had a plan.

For the life of me though, as I lay next to my sick grandson, two doors away from my dying husband with a womb void of life, I wanted to scream. There was no God. There couldn't be. What possible plan could He, if He existed, have for me out of the sadness and loss? There was no rhyme or reason.

The entire world was suffering.

If there was a God, did he just up and walk away, say, "I quit" and play billiard balls with some planets to cause the destruction?

Not only did I feel emotionally hollow and drained, the world quite simply felt abandoned.

By two p.m., Tag's fever was steadily high. He coughed uncontrollably, his little lungs fighting to break up and bring out whatever was blocking them. Fortunately he was out of it and slept.

The last thing he said to me was, "Tell me a story." He always said that.

Did I tell him I loved him? I was certain I did, I always did.

It was easy to tell when Sam pulled an all-nighter, falling asleep just as the weather was tolerable enough and sleeping late. Hence why we never saw him until the afternoon. I guessed he came over to check on me and Jeff. He was unprepared for the news he received.

The semi upbeat man was floored. Upon hearing Tag was sick, his face grew pale and he looked as if he took a bullet. He literally grabbed his chest and dropped to his knees at the bedside of Tag.

"Not my little guy," He grabbed Tag's hand. "My God is he fevered. Tag…Tag…"

"He hasn't responded all…"

"Hey… Sam…" Tag replied soft and slow. "Can't work today."

"It's okay, you just rest and get well."

Tag's lips were swollen from the fever and with a pout, he nodded and closed his eyes again.

Sam's face turned beet red and it looked as if every muscle around his mouth tensed up. He twitched his head to the right, wiped his hand under his nose and stood up. "What the fuck?" he said with angry emotion.

I couldn't speak. My throat was swollen. "I'm sorry."

"Something is not right. How did he get sick? We kept him away."

"Bill, Millie. We were around them." I said. "They were around others."

"You're not sick."

"Doesn't matter, some people get it some don't. Doctor Stanley said I am still at risk."

"But you don't care," he said.

"Not at all."

He placed his hand on the back of my head and brought his lips to my forehead. "I'm sorry. I am."

"I know."

"I came over to check on you and give news, but now is not the time."

"What news?"

Sam exhaled heavily, "I know you didn't want to move Jeff. But, Tess, those flames are gonna roll over those mountains and blast this town with a vengeance. By day after tomorrow, it will heat up."

"That doesn't make sense. A wall of fire and we aren't feeling it now."

Sam shrugged. "I don't know what to tell you. From what I heard on the radio, the flames will roll in. Heat will increase right before they get here and last transport leaves Glendale on the eighteenth at six in the morning. It's some sort of unnatural phenomenon how it's happening. Right now it is all still guessing."

I really didn't have a response. I took in his information, nodded and thanked him. I didn't know what to say. I didn't want to think about it.

We were being blasted by devastation any way you looked at it. Things were moving unexpectedly, unlike any science community could predict.

Maybe I was right in thinking that there was a God. Hearing the way things were playing out, the phrase unnatural phenomenon, made me think there was a God and more than likely, he was done with us.

THIRTY-ONE - SAILOR'S DELIGHT

In the little over thirty hours since my physical loss, my body began to feel better. I pulled some clothes from my bottom drawer. Something with a waist that had give, because my belly was still tender and swollen.

Dr. Stanley had returned to give us a quick lesson in intravenous. But Josh was well aware of how to do so, he learned in the service. After hooking up the shunt to Tag's arm, he ran an IV of fluids into him to keep him hydrated.

It was bad enough he was sick, he didn't need to suffer any more through dehydration.

Tag still lay in the same spot of the bed, his spot. He was on his side facing the door and Nicole sat next him, close to the bed, holding his hand and placing her face close to his.

She just stared at him. I could only imagine her thoughts, what went through her mind, her fears. Her pain. Yet, her face was calm and emotionless. In a sense I envied her. I wore my pain like a badge. One I couldn't hide.

I sat up in bed, needing to go check on Jeff. "I'm proud of you, Nicole."

"Don't be," she said with a weakened voice. "I have missed so much of his life because of my stupidity. And now... I'm never going to have the chance to share the rest of his life."

"He loves you," I told her. "He loves you so much." I stood and walked around to her side of the bed. "You are so strong right now. I don't know how you're doing it."

"I'm not, Marmie. I'm dying inside. Every ounce of me is dying inside."

"I leaned down, wrapping my arms around her. "I wish with all my heart there was something I could tell you, do for you, to take away the pain. None of this makes sense."

"It never will."

"You're right. It never will." She squeezed my arms,

After kissing her, I walked into the next bedroom. We had moved Jeff into there. He, like Tag was connected to an IV bag. There was horrible smell in the room, one I could not pinpoint. He slept in a medicated state, totally unaware, yet his body twitched and arms grabbed for his skin. I had placed socks over his hands to keep him from ripping open his flesh. The sores wouldn't heal and they spread across this body.

Did he even know we were losing Tag too?

I wanted to wake him and tell him, but he didn't need any more grief.

I checked the sheet on Jeff, then opened the window the widest it would go. Not that it would make a difference. The temperature didn't drop as it did the night before.

I needed some water, and knew there was some downstairs. I was just about to head that way when I heard the knock on the door.

Julie came out of her room. "Want me to get that?"

"No, I'm heading down. Go to sleep." I said and walked down the stairs.

Surprisingly, Reverend Ray was at the door. He held a box.

I pushed open the screen door and stepped out. "What brings you here?"

"I um, wanted to bring the rest of the saline solution for the IV's." He said and opened the screen door, placing the box directly inside. He nervously wiped his hands on his pants. "Thought you know, you and Jeff and..." he cleared his throat. "Tag would need them."

"Thank you. You don't need them?"

"I have what I need. I won't be needing any more come this time tomorrow."

"What do you mean?"

"Everyone is pretty sick at the church. I'll have no reason to stay when the last passes. Unless you need me to stay."

I shook my head. "No, you go. How...how can you be so sure they're going to die?"

"I've been watching this thing, this...flu for days. A good day and a half at the high fever and cough and then ... then the Lord takes them."

I scoffed a laugh and walked by him on the porch.

"Tess, I know you are in pain," he said. "I know you are carrying the burden but now is not the time to scoff in the face of faith."

"Faith," I laughed. "No, Ray, right now is the time to do so."

"Tess..."

"I had a great grandmother, she was ninety." I shrugged. "For as long as I could remember, even when she was younger, she would say, 'well, so and so is pregnant, might be my time to go'." I leaned against the porch railing. "The Lord gives a life and takes a life. That crossed my mind when my parents were killed in that home invasion. My cousin Claire had her twins the next day. The Lord gives, the Lord takes…seems as though lately, he keeps on taking."

He placed on his virtual preacher hat, and stepped to the edge of the porch. "I think of our ancestors before us and the trials and tribulations they faced. I imagine they were in this mindset. At such a loss when things around them, people around them died. Bubonic plague, Spanish Flu."

"I'm sure none of them faced something as epic as this."

"I'm sure it was to them, and I'm sure Noah would argue that."

Again, I released another ridiculing laugh. "Yeah, you think God's cleansing the earth."

"He might be."

"Yeah, well, if there is a God…"

"Tess, come on. You always have faith."

"I did. But now I wonder. And if he is cleansing the earth, then why?"

"Man does some things that aren't good."

"*Some* men are not good," I argued. "It's like wiping out a whole town because one person is a killer. It's judging the whole world."

"I don't think this is part of God's plan."

"If it's not then what is he waiting for? If He is so almighty, why hasn't he stepped in?"

"How do you know He hasn't? You can't give up."

"Are you saying there's a miracle around the corner?"

"You never know. Have faith."

"I lost my child, my husband is close to dying and so is Tag. If there's a miracle, it needs to come now."

"You can't put..." Suddenly Reverend Ray stopped talking and he moved to the edge of my porch staring out.

I was about to ask him to finish when I saw that his attention was drawn elsewhere. I walked to the edge of the porch to join him and that was when I saw what he did. What had taken the words from his mouth. The entire lower portion of the western sky was bright red.

Red sky at night sailors delight was the old saying. But that sky didn't scream delight, it screamed something more ominous. To me, it quite simply screamed...the end.

THIRTY-TWO - GOOD LIFE

July 16

There was no way to count how many times I had heard someone tell me, "I'll sleep when I'm dead." That never made sense to me, until I pushed the limits of what I believed was my own mortality. Without a doubt, I felt as if I were dying.

I wasn't well. I didn't have energy or passion.

Sleep wasn't on the cards for me and I made Nicole get some sleep. She did, laying next to her son in my bed. I took her chair and went back and forth between Tag and Jeff. Trying to divide my time equally, trying to get what I could from the time I had left with both of them.

It didn't make sense.

Jeff arrived back home sick and I watched him slowly deteriorate over the last couple days.

Tag was another story.

Healthy and fine one second, running around and the next he was in some sort of fever limbo. Opening his eyes only briefly and giving us just a taste of him before he slipped away again. There was a sense of it being surreal, as if I were waiting for the switch to flip, Tag to say he was feeling better and then all would be right with the world.

That was my fantasy.

Somewhere just after the light of morning, Jeff entered a rare lucid state. He looked bad, sounded and smelled bad. Despite everything, his spirits were good. Another reason I didn't want to tell him about Tag.

Because of the orange hue he asked if it were evening. I told him it wasn't, he accepted that then asked me to pack a pipe.

"Jeff, really?"

"Yeah," he said. "I don't have much time, Tess. I'm fighting it. I feel that."

"Maybe you are getting better."

"Nah, can you get my pipe. I think I want to meet my maker stoned."

"Par for the course," I told him. "You met everyone else in your life stoned."

"I did, didn't I?" He smiled.

The smile was good to see.

I had brought his stash up from the weed room and packed his pipe for him. I had to light it; his fingers were too weak to work the lighter.

He hit his pipe, coughed, and then hit it again. "I had a good life with you, Tess. Tell me you had a good life, too."

"I had a good life, too," I said. "I'm sorry that I told you I was so unhappy."

"I knew you weren't. I just think you didn't know what happiness was."

He was right. I did now. I was happy. I just didn't recognize it. I had it all. And now I was losing it all.

There was an abominable sense of sadness and loss in that room, one that wasn't dampened by his marijuana induced state. For the first time in days he asked for water. He said he was thirsty and I was glad to oblige.

"I'll be right back," I told him. "Want me to take that?" I asked in reference to the pipe.

"Nah, I'm good."

I made my way to the kitchen and when I entered, Josh was there along with Julie. She held Liam on her hip. Immediately, I felt bad.

"Julie, honey, I am so sorry, I didn't mean to make you take care of the baby."

"It's okay." She approached the counter. Her eyes were red and she looked sad, almost scared. "Marmie, please don't get mad."

"What is it?"

"I know Daddy is sick. I know Tag is sick. But…it's happening soon, Marmie. Are….are we going to leave?"

My heart sunk.

I had been concentrating on those who were dying and didn't stop to think about those still alive. My daughter was still alive and was expressing that she didn't want that to change.

My eyes lifted to Josh. "Is everything ready to go?"

"Yes," he nodded. "Last transport leaves less than two days from right now."

"They're taking people east," Julie said. "Trying to help people survive. If we run out of gas we need to allow ourselves time to walk. I know you don't want to think about it. But I have to know if we are leaving."

I breathed out. "Then what?" I asked. "We pack up, we make a transport, we go east, then what?"

Josh simply replied. "Live."

To me, at that second, all I could think about was if it was worth living. The world was going to struggle to survive. Battling illness, the unnatural phenomenon that was taking place. If we lived, how long would it be? What kind of life would it be?

Did I have the right to make that decision for my daughter, Josh or Liam?

Just as I was about to express my feelings, I heard Jeff call my name.

It was a calm, rational call. Like he had done many times. Almost as if he were calling me to take a look at something.

"Tess."

"Excuse me." I said and after grabbing water, I made my way back upstairs.

When I entered the room, Jeff was laying on his back, He lifted the pipe for me to take it.

I reached for it.

"Tess, can you get the girls?"

"What for?" I asked.

"I…I want to say goodbye."

Fingers holding that pipe, my eyes locked on to his. The color of his pupils had gone and his eyes had taken on a grayish appearance.

"I'm ready to go," he said.

My stomach twitched and my head immediately filled with blood. I could hear it rushing through my ears.

"Get the girls, Tess."

As I pulled my hand back, he grabbed it,

"I love you," he said.

"I love you, too, Jeff." I placed the pipe on the table and walked to the door. I paused to look back at him.

He rested back, yet didn't close his eyes. In fact he looked as if he fought to keep them open. It was time, I sensed it and knew it. There was a foreboding essence that lingered in the house.

His short span of hard suffering was about to come to an end.

The first person I sought was Julie. She didn't want me to hear what she was discussing with Josh. That was obvious, she immediately silenced and looked awkward when I walked in.

"Marmie?" She questioned and looked at me.

"Let Josh take Liam. Come say goodbye to your father."

Julie, my strong Julie, whimpered upon hearing my words and then I walked back upstairs.

Before Julie could get there, I walked into Jeff's room and to him. I grabbed his hand. "I'm going to get Nicole, then sit with Tag so you can be with the girls. Okay?"

He nodded. "Thank you for our years."

I leaned down and kissed him softly, then brought my lips to his ears and whispered. "I'm not far behind you. Wait for me. Look for me."

He exhaled heavily and tightened the grip on my hand. I felt his strength, I felt his sadness, and then as hard as it was, I pulled my hand from his.

I knew. I just knew as I stood in the doorway looking back at him, that it would be the last time I looked at my husband alive.

Julie walked into the room as I left and I went back to my room. I absolutely hated the fact that I had to disturb Nicole. She was sound asleep holding her son.

"Nic," I whispered to her. "Hey, wake up."

She opened her eyes.

"Baby, go say goodbye to Daddy."

She immediately jumped up. Her eyes widened with fear.

"Go on," I said. "I'll sit with Tag."

"Don't you want to be there?"

"You go. Go on."

We exchanged places, and I slipped in bed next to Tag. His body was hot, so hot making it painful and emotionally unbearable to hold him. But I did. I clutched him against me, kissing him constantly as he slept.

It wasn't long at all. I knew it was done, it was over, I sensed it and then I heard the crying, the "Daddy." coming from Julie.

The sobs carried to me. Hearing them, I closed my eyes tighter and scooted closer to Tag. Their father was gone, my husband, I felt and heard their grief.

In my mind, quietly and privately, from the other room, I held on to Tag and said goodbye to my husband.

THIRTY-THREE - CHOICE

We watched Reverend Ray drive by just as we tossed the last of the dirt over Jeff in a shallow grave under the increasingly growing red sky. Josh wiped the sweat from his brow. He was at the end. Could he push forward? I didn't know. Julie had calmed down but was on edge, and Nicole stayed inside with Tag.

Jeff's farewell consisted of bringing him outside, and doing what we could to bury him. The heat was increasing by the minute.

It wouldn't matter. In two days time, Falcon's Way would be a burnt wasteland.

Jeff and everything else we loved would be ashes.

I appreciated all that Josh had done. He paused to watch Reverend Ray drive until he was completely out of sight. I knew he was the last one. Other than us, no one remained. Josh had made a sweep of town.

We were the last.

I knew, with death all around us, it was time for me to make a decision on life. That was reiterated when Sam pulled me aside and told me, "Tess, we're out of time."

My decision had been made.

"Mommy, no." Julie argued with me. "No."

For the first time I could truly recall, I was flexing my matriarchal muscles. I ignored her pleas in the kitchen and faced Josh. "Finish taking everything out. Don't forget the wagon. For each second we waste, is a second we can change our minds."

179

"Yes, Ma'am." Josh replied.

"Tess, listen," Sam said. "We can wait. I want to wait."

"Wait?" I questioned with a hint of sarcasm. "That's morbid. We are we gonna do, sit around, wait for Tag to pass, pack on up and caravan away. That's not gonna happen."

"There's the last transport…"

"Last. Keyword." I held up my finger. "There isn't enough gas to get to Phoenix or Glendale, that's a lot of walking. We can't take that chance on making the last transport. The last transport cannot be the goal it has to be the backup plan. We waited too long. It's time to go. We make the goodbye quick."

"Mommy, please," Julie pleaded.

"I love you, baby, I love you so much." I laid my hand on her face. "That's why we are doing this. It'll be okay. It will."

Julie who rarely cried was sobbing. I attributed a lot of that to the overwhelming sadness she was feeling over her father.

She did not realize that Jeff would be pissed at me if I didn't do everything I could to make sure his children lived. I was implementing the plan to do just that.

"Finish helping Josh," I told Julie. "When you're done, then we say our goodbyes. Sam?" I held my hand out to him. "Come with me to tell Nicole."

Nicole was still in the same spot, sitting next to the bed. Her hands cupped over Tag's, her face close to his.

She must have heard us walk in. She didn't look, only said, "He hasn't opened his eyes since this morning."

"He's fighting it," I said, walking up to her. "His body is just fighting."

"Am I a terrible mother?" she asked.

"No, God, why would you ask that?"

"Aside the fact that I missed a lot of his life…am I terrible mother because I resolved myself that no miracle, no amount of hoping and praying is going to save my son. I'm losing him."

I lowered my head. "It doesn't make you terrible. It makes you realistic. I envy you."

"Marmie, I keep telling myself, he's sick. He's sleeping so he's not feeling it. He's being spared the hard life we all have to face. Am I wrong? Am I telling myself that to make it feel okay?"

Sam spoke up. "You tell yourself whatever you need to tell yourself. You hear? I found myself last night being so thankful my wife passed away and didn't have to face this. Whatever it takes, you do."

I sat on the bed at Tag's feet, facing Nicole as my hand rested on his legs. "Nicole, listen to me."

She lifted her eyes.

"You know I love Tag more than life itself," I said. "You know I love you and Julie just as much. Daddy, the baby, Tag, this world sadly is going to go on without them. You and Julie need to be part of that world. You are the future. What I am going to tell you is going to be hard. But listen to me fully."

"Go on."

I placed my hand on hers. "Baby, we're out of time. I know we all want to stay with Tag, but we run the chance that if we do, we miss the transport and any chance of surviving."

"I don't care."

"I do." My voice cracked. "I want you to take this moment, hold him, tell him you love him, then you need to go."

"No." She blasted me emotionally. "What? Are you insane? I am not leaving him. I am not leaving him here to die alone."

"He's not gonna be alone."

Nicole stared at me.

"I will be here with him. I will stay until the very end. I will hold him, and not let go."

She swiped her hand across her face. "If anyone stays. I do."

"If you stay, you will die."

"He's my child!"

"And you are mine! Julie is my child. I already lost one in this world; please don't make me face losing another. Tag will live on as long as you are there to carry his memory with you."

"Why don't we take him? Just bring us with him. Some of the transports are taking the ill."

"Is that fair to Tag?" I lowered my face to hers. "This is breaking my heart. Killing me. But is it fair to him to take him with us, carry him when we have to walk? Is it fair to him to leave this earth from the back of a truck or the side of the road? Instead of here, right here, surrounded by everything he knew and loved. If we leave and bring him, who is that for? Him? It's for us. So why do it?"

Clenching her fist, Nicole cried her words. "One more moment. One last moment. I want it all. I want every second I can."

"I know you do. You deserve it. But he and your father deserve to have you live on."

"What about you, Marmie?"

"Knowing you and Julie will be all right is what I want. Besides, someone has to keep your father in line." I sniffled. "Think about this, Nicole. I know this is hard. Think about it. There's a little boy out there that lost it all. He needs a strong mother now. It doesn't replace Tag. But it gives you a purpose. It also doesn't make you wrong for leaving, it makes you right for living." I planted my lips to the top of her head and stood. "Take your moment."

In the silence of the room, I grabbed Sam's hand and we walked from the bedroom.

Walked away listening to the sounds of Nicole weeping.

It would not have surprised me in the least if Nicole changed her mind at the last second and said that she was staying behind. I was mentally prepared for that. If she did, I would say my goodbyes to the both of them, and as heartbreaking as it would be, I'd have to leave. There was no way I could leave Julie alone in this world without any family.

I wanted Nicole with her. They were both young and strong enough to carry on in life.

After giving Josh my instructions to take care of Julie and Liam, my daughter held tight to me. Her arms wrapped around my waist, her head to my chest and she squeezed.

"Don't stay behind, please," Julie begged. "Please. I love you. Please."

"I don't want to leave Tag. He's too weak to go. And Nicole … and you will be just fine."

She shook her head.

"Listen to me," I lifted her chin. "I need you to live. I need you to live a long life." I sniffed in hard. "Statistically speaking…"

Julie quickly glanced up at me.

I had thrown her own stock phrase at her.

"You have a better shot at life than I do. I'm sick, Julie, the baby, the loss, it took a toll on me. Just go and you look back once, when you are safely out of town."

"I can't."

"You will."

I was trying to be strong, I really was. Holding on to her, projecting that I was brave, when in actuality, I was scared to death. Scared of what would happen, sad that my daughter was going to be without her parents. After our long embrace, she slipped by me to say her own goodbyes to Tag. He had been such a part of our lives, every single day since Nicole was incarcerated.

Josh approached while everyone was in the room with Tag.

"We're ready," he said. "Truck is ready to go. We should hit walking distance by nightfall."

"You have the flashlights and radio?"

"I do."

I stepped to him and embraced him. "Thank you. I hope you find your family."

"I'm sure they caught a transport."

Julie came back out of the room and grabbed on to me again.

She repeatedly told me she loved me. I knew this, it hurt to hear. It killed me to know how much it was going to pain her. It's what had to be done.

"Sweetie, did you take all the pictures?"

"I did."

"Go. I love you. Go now." I raised my eyes to Josh. "Take her."

Julie wouldn't let go of me.

"Come on, Julie," Josh beckoned. "Let's go."

"No, it's my mother. No."

I closed my eyes tightly. Grabbing her arms from around my neck, 'be strong for me, please." Cupping her face in my hands, I kissed her one last time.

She slipped from my final touch and never took her eyes from me as Josh moved her down the hall. Once she was out of sight, I walked into my bedroom.

Of all the rooms in the house, that one was the most evident of what was happening in the world. It had the prettiest orange glow about it.

Sam was in front of the window. He had placed a small air conditioning unit in there. He stood and turned around. "Generator will run for a few hours. Two more gas cans there for you," he said. "It'll make things tolerable for you both."

"Thank you."

"Don't know how long it will work with the heat rising."

"I know."

He walked up to me, grabbed my hands and placed a set of keys in it.

"Sam?"

"My car is in the port. Ten gallons are in the trunk, extra gas. A few bottles of water. Ignition is a bitch. For some unknown reason you have to hit it three times before she'll start. Always called it my poor man's car alarm."

"Sam why are you giving me your keys?"

"In case, you know, you change your mind and there's still time."

"I won't change my mind, but thank you." I placed the keys on the nightstand. "I'm staying behind for a reason."

"You never know, maybe that reason is your supposed to wait for a miracle."

I wanted to scoff at that, but I didn't. Sam was a good man and was serious about what he was saying. His goodbye to Tag at that second was brief. He had done a longer one earlier. He embraced me and headed to the door.

"Thank you for taking care of my family," I said. "Thank you so much."

"We're all family now, Tess. We're all family and it is my honor and privilege."

Then...I looked at Sam one last time before he disappeared from that doorframe.

The final moment.

Nicole stood slowly, bringing the sheet over Tag. "You'll need this. It's gonna get cold, baby," she said, then kissed him again. "Mommy loves you so much." Then she grasped onto me and held me. "I love you, Marmie."

"I love you, too."

"Tell him...tell him every second you can how much we love him. Okay? Please."

"I will. I promise. He will know."

Saying goodbye while knowing there would never be a reunion was a difficult and awkward thing to do. We didn't want to let go, yet knew it had to be done.

She stole one more moment with Tag, and then looked back to me as she stood in the doorway. Her eyes glanced to her son. "Goodbye my precious one."

Head lowered, Nicole walked out.

I heard the sound of her running from the house. I suppose so she wouldn't change her mind. From the bedroom window, I watched for as long as I could as they drove away. Then I fired up the generator, put the small window unit on cool, and sat on the bed next to Tag.

We were alone. Not even the hum of the air conditioning and generator could cover up the feel of empty in the home.

It permeated the air reiterating that the world had moved forward. By choice, Tag and I were now alone in that part of the country, alone, isolated to face the inevitable end.

THIRTY-FOUR – STORY

I had become quite proficient in changing Tag's IV bag. I firmly believed that constant, slow flowing of liquid was the reason he was still alive. There were only two bags remaining. Unfortunately, they wouldn't get us through the next twenty-four hours. Though I highly doubted, we would be around.

It was all too reminiscent, in a bigger way of course, of the wild fire seasons back when Jeff and I lived closer to the coast. During the season the fires would burn in the hills a distance from our home. Slowly and surely they made their way closer as firefighters and volunteers gave their all to battle the blaze and neighbors tried with diligence to save their homes by watering the roofs.

When the wildfires would close in and evacuation orders arrived. When a mere day or two separated you from the flames, there was a smell of 'burning' that lingered in the air as the temperature increased. One time, Jeff and I stayed longer at our home than we should have. It was hot and the entire horizon was nothing but a huge orange wall of fire.

I imagined on a grander scale, the devastation that would roll through Falcon's Way.

The sun set, I was certain, but it was hard to tell because the fires lit up the sky. It was close. Too close. Peering out Julie's window gave me the western vantage point and the ability to see the orange sky. It was red the evening before and even more so as we lived that last night.

I was getting tired and I sipped on a bottle of water. I remembered Sam telling me that radiation levels would rise, but it didn't matter to me.

I lost the baby, my husband, and was on the verge of losing Tag. I was there when he took his first breath and sadly I would be there when he took his last. The only saving grace for me was that I would not feel the horrendous sadness for very long. Death would consume me and take away all the pain.

Perhaps it was selfish of me not to want to live. But I didn't. I honestly didn't know if I was strong enough to carry on with the pain of the losses.

I had dampened a cloth and just finished wiping down Tag, when surprisingly, he opened his eyes. I lay on my side, facing him as he looked at me. The whites of his eyes were red, his little lips puffy and he exuded an aroma of fever.

Taking the cloth I moistened his lips as he watched me.

"I love you," I told him.

"Love you." He puckered as he swallowed. "My throat hurts."

"I know."

"I'm cold."

"It's the fever." The small air conditioner had given a bit of relief and enough that I had to pull the blanket up over him. "Better?"

He nodded and inched my way, I pulled him closer to me, kissing him, and tensing up inside when I felt how hot his skin was.

"Tell me a story, Marmie."

How many times had he said that to me? Hearing him say it broke my heart because I wouldn't hear him say it again.

Tell me a story, Marmie.

I pulled him as close as I could to me, cuddling and holding him.

Tell me a story, Marmie.

A story. A story about beautiful things. Sunrises and songs. A mother who loved him so much and a family that adored him more than life itself. I would tell him about the joy he brought and the life ahead, a great life with every wish he ever had, coming true.

Tell me a story, Marmie.

I would.

I would tell him one for as long as I could and as long as he listened. I would tell him a story, the last story, I would ever share with Tag.

THIRTY-FIVE – THREE TIMES

July 17

I fought to stay awake, hold Tag, listen to him breathe, but my exhaustion took over and sleep happened whether I wanted it to or not. After a few hours, three things caused me to wake up. The bright red color to the room, the heat against my eyes and the sudden silence from the defunct air conditioning unit.

I shifted my eyes to the window and saw the brightness out there. It wouldn't be long.

Then as I came to, I felt it.

There was no heat emanating from Tag. No scorching skin. He was cool.

No.

My heart sunk and daggers of pain shot through every fiber in my body.

I didn't want to fall asleep, I had wanted to be awake, to hear that last breath, and be there as he left this earth. My being was crushed. I had failed myself and Tag. I wanted to scream. In my agony, I grabbed for him, pulling him closer and into my body. Squeezing him with every emotion I had.

Death could not come soon enough for me.

I had lost what I believed the final breath that held me to life.

Tag.

"Marmie, you're squishing me," the tiny voice peeped out.

Was I imagining it? Hearing things?

Instantaneously, I lost my breath pulled back and looked. Tag's eyes were open. He blinked. My hands ran about his face, then neck and arms.

He was cool.

His fever had broken.

He had either beat the flu or never had it. Either way, I looked at the window and realized a mistake had been made. A huge mistake and I had to change it.

A huge sense of urgency hit me, and with an "Oh my God," of gratefulness, I kissed him, sat up, swung my legs out of bed and put on my shoes. I stood, racing over to the corner where I had thrown his clothes two days earlier, stuck his shirt in my back pocket and grabbed his shoes.

"Marmie?"

My hands shook as I put them on sloppily.

After, I lifted his arm and carefully, but quickly pulled the IV from him, and wrapped the cloth I used to wipe him down, around his arm.

"What's happening?" he asked.

I didn't answer. I didn't have time to answer. I'm sure he was confused, and I would explain things to him later. I swept him up into my arms, told him to hold tight, and with one swift motion, I turned and swept those keys, Sam had left, from the nightstand and bolted from the bedroom.

I had wished for death to come, now I begged it to stay away. Keep away.

Give us a chance.

I took nothing else but Tag from the house and paused only a second on the porch to look at the sky. The flames in the distance were evident and close. The swirling orange blasted waves of heat at us. It was a good thing I put on my shoes, because everything was hot to the touch. I could feel the heat coming from the pavement as I rushed across the street to Sam's.

Sure enough his car was parked in the carport front end out and ready to go.

It was unlocked and I opened the passenger's door. There was a box on the seat and I knocked it to the floor, spilling the bottles of water and other contents. I set Tag in the seat and forgoing the belt I closed the door.

I rushed to get in the driver's side. My hands trembled so badly I couldn't get the key in the ignition of the old car.

'Please,' I thought, 'please let us just get out of here and away from the fire. Please.'

I turned the key.

Nothing.

"Shit!" I hit the steering wheel and turned the key.

It didn't make a sound. It was dead. Had the heat killed it?

My only other option was to grab Tag and run, just run until I couldn't go any further.

One more time. Give it one more try.

I turned it again.

"Damn it."

"You have to beat it," Tag said. "Sam does."

Beat it. Oh my God.

"Hit it three times," Sam had told me. "Don't ask me why."

On Tag's words, the memory of what Sam said, and a whole lot of hope, I banged the ignition three times and turned the key.

The engine started.

I squealed with delight, and threw the car in gear. Wasting no more time, I hightailed it from the carport and into our street.

I kept going and I didn't once look back.

THIRTY-SIX - ASSESSING

I didn't stop until I knew I was a good distance away. Until the orange in the sky faded enough for me to feel secure. I had sworn Sam said he had a full tank of gas, but that wasn't the case looking at the gauge. Maybe it was and his old car was just a guzzler.

I pulled over to catch my breath,

Tag had not said much. It was as much a whirlwind for him as it was for me. To make sure it wasn't a dream, I reached over and touched him. He was cool.

I exhaled.

Then the guilt hit me.

I had given up. I had no faith. Bill our neighbor swore he had a bacterial infection and I listened to Dr. Stanley. By doing so, and giving up, I nearly condemned Tag to death one way or another.

Thankfully, we made it out of town in time. We had a shot at the last transport. It was leaving Glendale at six a.m. Not only was Glendale nearly three hundred miles away, I didn't have a clue where in Glendale the transport was.

I needed time. Time to get there, walk if we had to and find the transport place. I hoped the gas would get us close enough to give us enough time.

If it didn't, I wasn't giving up. I'd find away. I had to. I had Tag.

"Where are we?" Tag asked.

I didn't know how to answer. "Outside Falcon's Way."

"Where are we going?"

"Tag...how do you feel?" I asked and turned to face him, changing the subject.

"Better."

"Good. Good." I ran my hand down his face. "You were very sick."

"Where is everybody?"

I took a moment and a breath. "Tag, you know how it is hot? Well, it's getting hotter and dangerous. Your mom, Julie, Josh …"

"And Sam?"

"Yes, and Sam. They went ahead to get to a safe place. You were sick, so I waited until you got better."

"Good thing I got better, huh?"

"Good thing. Now, I just need to take a second and look at the supplies we have. We need supplies in case we have to walk."

I turned my attention to the items that spilled on the floor. A few bottles of water and packs of crackers. It wasn't much. I gathered them up and put them in the box. Maybe we'd be lucky and pass an abandoned store.

"Sam's fishing backpack is behind your seat," Tag said. "He keeps it there."

I turned around enough to look and sure enough, there it was. A blue knapsack. I opened it. Inside was a small blanket, flashlight, and half a roll of toilet paper. Matches, a half pint of whiskey and a few other things. I shoved the water we did have along with the crackers in the knapsack and placed it on the floor in front of Tag's feet.

The small amount of supplies would suffice to get us to the transport. If we needed more beyond that, I would worry about it when the time came.

Right then, my focus was on moving forward. After a brief stop on the highway, putting the stash of gas in the tank, we continued on our journey to Glendale.

THIRTY-EIGHT – CATCHING BREATH

Tag had fallen asleep pretty quickly in the car. I worried he was relapsing, especially when he'd cough occasionally. But that was only my fear. His fever stayed away and he was just recovering.

He didn't ask many questions, that was a good thing because I didn't know how to answer them.

Halfway through our journey we came across Dispon's Oasis. A truck stop diner and gas station. It was empty, not a car or soul in sight.

I kept thinking about the transport and how it was taking us east. The east coast wasn't close, the journey would be long and what if we were responsible for our own well being and survival.

A few bottles of water and crackers weren't going to cut it.

I pulled right up to the door. We needed to stop for a few minutes and see if they had anything. When I opened the door for Tag, I realized he was still very weak. His little legs wobbled and he lost his balance.

"I'm sorry, Marmie," he said.

"No, don't be. I'll carry you."

He was half my size, but somehow I didn't pay attention to whether he was heavy or not, His legs tried to latch on to my waist, but they kept slipping and dangling over my knees.

The door was locked, the diner shut down. I put Tag back in the car while I sought out the tire rod from the trunk and busted the door window.

When I cleared a safe path, I lifted Tag again.

Once inside I set him down. Immediately he eyed the rack of goodies by the register.

"Can I have candy? I'm hungry."

"Absolutely," I grabbed a candy bar for him. It was soft and half melted from the heat. After unwrapping it, I grabbed a paper napkin and handed them both to Tag. "Eat slowly."

It was eerily empty in that diner. There were no plates of food, half eaten meals. It had been closed for days. Not much longer because there wasn't a lot of dust.

I took out what I didn't need from Sam's backpack, and put in what I could. Searching around that diner, I was able to get another pack from the tiny gift shop. I could have taken a lot more water, but I had to keep in mind the weight of the packs.

Tag and I could ration water.

I shoved boxes of cereal, granola bars, and items that would keep and not melt.

Of course batteries went in the bag as well.

We took a break in that diner, not too long, but enough time to get my bearings and get some food in us.

Because I didn't know when we'd see or use a real one again, Tag and I used the bathroom and then, refreshed and full, we took off again.

We'd get there, I was confident. Even if we missed the transport, we were better off than staying in Falcon's Way. Whether our journey ended in Glendale or not, I knew everything was going to be okay. I'd make it be okay. I had Tag. He was alive and he gave me reason to keep going.

THIRTY-NINE - HEADLIGHTS

July 18

I was hopeful. We were doing well. Then just as the sign appeared that told us thirty-seven miles to Phoenix, the car sputtered out the last bit of gas and died. I was glad that it was in the later portion of the day. At least the heat would be more tolerable, if that were possible.

Stay hydrated, steady and focused.

That was my plan.

I could do it. I could do thirty-seven miles.

I didn't take into account, the two backpacks and the fact that I had to carry Tag most of the way.

With thoughts only on getting there, I kept walking. Once and a while, Tag would walk, it gave me a break. Then he'd wear down, his legs would give out and we'd stop.

Once the sun had set, it was easier. But it was still unbearably hot.

I kept focused. My mind spun with thoughts. At first, they were negative. If we made the transport, then what? What was next? They would move us east? Would we even find our family? Would we spend the next weeks or months, possibly years looking for them?

The thought of that scared me.

Then it was easily replaced with the thoughts of Nicole. How happy she would be to see her son. How thrilled Julie would be to find out we hadn't died.

Those thoughts kept me going.

I had no idea what time it was. As long as the sky stayed dark we were good. We had to stop a lot. Both for me and Tag. Thirty-seven miles when neither of us was well was a difficult task. As we moved on, I felt my body weaken. I no longer walked a straight and steady line, with or without Tag in my arms. I grew fearful of dying. What if I died? What if I collapsed? Then what would happen to Tag?

He fell asleep in my arms and I found myself stopping more frequently. The last time I stopped, was the one that told me I was done. I sat down and it took everything I had to get back up. When I did, I noticed not only the outline of Phoenix, but the sky was lighting.

There was no way we were making that last transport.

Time for a Plan B. Use the walking to think of that, instead of failure in getting there. How would we survive? Head east.

Stay ahead of the flames.

Surely there were others.

My legs began to fold with each step. I was barely able to walk. My stomach cramped, back hurt, arms ached. Each time I adjusted Tag in my arms, I felt myself starting to fall.

Just when I thought, 'We aren't making it anyhow, we might as well stop,' I heard it.

Beep.

A honk of a horn, sound of a motor and when I looked up, a truck rolled by me.

I didn't even have the energy to scream out.

I didn't need to. A hundred feet up the road, the brake lights lit and then the truck backed up.

I stepped out of the way in case some sadistic person wanted to run us down. Instead, the truck stopped.

The driver was a thickset man in his forties, Hispanic. He leaned to the door and pushed it open.

"You trying to catch the last transport?" he asked.

I exhaled, nearly in tears from his rescue. "Yes."

"Get in." He pushed the door wider. "I will take you."

"Oh God, thank you."

It was awkward trying to get into the truck, backpacks on both shoulders and Tag in my arms. I was scared to put him in first. What if the driver took off? Then he reassured my faith in humanity by placing the truck in gear, stepping out and helping me in. I placed the bags on the floor and kept Tag in my arms.

Suddenly my exhaustion left. I was exhilarated with hope.

"Thank you, thank you so much," I told him.

"You're welcome. Luis," he said. "My name is Luis."

"Tess," I introduced myself. "This is Tag. His real name is Steven."

"Is he sick?"

Before I could answer, Tag groaned out. "Not anymore."

"He was," I said. "He's better now."

"I am not sure we will make the last transport." He reached over and lifted a transistor radio. "If we do not, I have enough gas, we can try to catch it. Or keep going."

"I have supplies."

"Me, too."

"Do you know where it is?"

"The transport?" he asked. "Yes, at the arena in Glendale. That is the last one. Last radio transmission I heard said not many people were left."

202

"Why are you so late?" I asked. "And trust me, I am so glad you were."

"Long story," he said. "You?"

"Long story as well."

Luis stared forward for a moment, then said. "My wife was very ill. I stayed with her. I was not leaving, but changed my mind at the last moment after she passed."

"I'm sorry for your loss. I stayed back for the same reason. My husband died, but this little guy, he got better." I looked down to Tag. "And it was a mad dash. I didn't think I'd be doing this. I thought we would die."

"Me as well," he said. "But when faced against the odds, when faced with death, suddenly we fight for our right to live. This mad dash is our fight."

"Will we win?" I asked.

Luis hesitated before answering. "We already have."

FORTY - LAST TRANSPORT

In the short span of time that I rode in the truck with Luis, I learned a lot about him. He didn't mention the distance we were from Glendale, but he said he was impressed with how far I had walked. He had seen our car on the side of the road and was looking out for us.

"It didn't look as if it had been there for long," he said. "I slowed down to get a good look and kept an eye out."

"We are so glad you did."

His story was very similar to mine. He had resolved himself to dying. Having lost his mother and father, then his wife. Luis told the exact same story, he was lying in bed with his wife, her final hours. He was watching the sky grew more orange, and then she passed.

Something clicked in him. It wasn't like he was waiting on her death to run, he hadn't planned on that. But the second she died he changed his mind.

"I don't know what happened, but suddenly I wanted to live," he said. "I wanted to see what was going to become of this world, hard or not."

He drove quickly, glancing at the old wristwatch he wore. Never did he mention the time, but I knew we were cutting it close.

"Keep an eye out," he said. "For any movement, any vehicles. Some are trains that are taking people, some are trucks."

"Do you know anything else?" I asked. "Anything at all."

"No, I'm sorry. Maybe they will give information when we get there."

When we get there. In my mind, it was more *'if'* we get there.

Phoenix was a ghost down. Not a soul on the street, no movement, no cars. It was so dead, not even a breeze swept up and moved the litter.

Luis' madman driving skills picked up, squealing the tires as he pushed the limits to get to the Arena.

He knew, I knew when it was in sight ....we had missed the transport.

Empty.

He slowed down as he drove across the entrance plaza, pulled directly to the doors and then put the truck in park.

"I'm sorry," he said.

"No. No, don't apologize. You tried. We'd still be on the highway. What time is it? How long did we miss it by?"

His lips puckered and he shifted his eyes to his watch. "Six fifteen."

I exhaled. In actuality, we probably had already missed it when he grabbed us on the side of the road.

"I have a generator in back. A small one," he said. "There will be lots of places we can get supplies. We can siphon gas, pump it from the reserves at stations. We can make it east."

"Then that's what we'll do."

He nodded. "And the transports are moving many people. Which means they will stop for breaks. We will run into one of them. We stay ahead of the flames we stay alive."

"I'm in. We're in."

"I'm gonna go inside and check to see if there is any information. Perhaps they posted a notice for those who missed the transport."

"Good idea."

He opened the truck door and stepped out. I watched Luis walk to the door, look around, then open it.

It was warm in the truck, Tag stirred in my arms, and I figured we'd step out and get some air.

"Wanna go outside?" I asked Tag. "Wait for Luis?"

Tag nodded and peeped out a 'yes'.

I removed Tag from my lap, opened the door and hopped down. Then I grabbed him. I was hopeful Luis would find information, but I wasn't counting on it. I was however, confident that we would make it east. There was no doubt in my mind. Not that I wouldn't have made it east on my own, I was just grateful that Luis happened upon us and I didn't have to do it alone.

Tag's head rested on my shoulder. He was tired, worn out. From a death bed to a mad dash, it took its toll on the boy.

"A man," he said.

"Yes, Luis, he'll be right back." I kept my eyes on the door waiting for him to come out.

Then I saw it, a reflection in the glass doors. Someone was approaching us from behind. I could clearly see he had a rifle.

My heart pounded.

"Are you looking for the last transport?" he called out.

I spun around and wheezed out a huge sigh of relief when I saw a male soldier.

"Yes. Yes we were," I answered. "But we missed it."

"No, you actually didn't." He pointed back. "We stopped about three blocks back. Very few people are on the bus and I came back for one last sweep."

Emotionally I gasped out "Thank you for doing one last sweep," and with Tag in my arms, I gave the soldier my best embrace.

He chuckled. "Good hearted as I am. I wanted to go. But some crazy guy on the bus made us check one more time. Said he saw a pickup flying in on the highway. Damned if he wasn't right." He pointed to Luis' truck. "If you're ready, we can head over."

"My friend … he's checking the arena."

"Stay put. Gather your stuff," he said. "You look pretty beat. I'll go search for him."

"Thank you. Thank you so much."

As the solider walked away, before getting our supplies, I grasped and squeezed Tag. "We did it. We made it."

We ended up giving Craig, the soldier a ride back to the transport. He had walked the three blocks. I will never forget Luis' face when he emerged from the arena with the soldier. It was so happy, and this newly found friend embraced me as if he had known me for years.

The transport was a gray school bus. Another soldier was at the door when we pulled up.

"Oh, he was right." The other soldier said. "He did see a truck."

"Tell me about it," Craig replied. At the bus door they took our names and gave us a bracelet with a number on it. "Don't lose that. That's how we are keeping track of all refugees." He placed a bracelet on

Tag. "He's one number after you," Craig said. "Not that you'll get separated, but just so know."

I was number, 56,877.

He then instructed us to take our things and get on the bus. It was a long journey.

Luis carried my backpacks because I still carried Tag. But as we approached the steps Tag wanted to walk. I placed him down but kept him right in front of me. We followed Luis onto the bus. Craig was right. It was pretty empty.

"Where is he?" I asked Craig who was behind me. "Show the guy who made you look. I wanted to thank him."

"Can't miss him. Right in the back."

Luis blocked my view and I peered around the right of him to check out the stranger. When I did, my heart pounded out of control and for the first time in days, I genuinely smiled.

It was Sam.

He peered out the window and before I could call his name he spotted me.

"Son of a bitch." He shrieked out and stood. "You did it. You made it. I knew it."

Luis turned around and looked at me. "You know him?"

"That's Sam. He left me his car."

Sam appeared impatient for us to get back there. He stood bouncing back and forth. But somehow, I believed he didn't know 'you' was actually 'we'. Upon that realization, I leaned down, lifted Tag.

Tag called out. "Sam!"

Sam's eyes widened and he fell backwards. I swore and feared he had a heart attack at the shock of seeing Tag.

It was a lot for him. His hands went to his face and I heard a slight whimper come from him. Sliding his fingers across his face, Sam peered upwards and mouthed the words, 'thank you'.

Luis slipped with the supplies into the seat in front of Sam and I bolted the remaining distance with Tag.

At that moment, Sam stood, arms extended and grabbed onto Tag. His murmured 'Oh my God,' over and over as he clutched Tag and plastered him with grateful kisses.

Then he reached to me and brought me into him. Sam was crying.

The reunion was awesome, but the bus jolted and we were told to take our seats. We did. Tag sat on Sam's lap.

"Where are the girls? Liam? Josh?" I asked.

"They are on the New Haven Transport. That's the final destination. This one I don't know where it's going, but I'm told we should be able to get to New Haven."

"How will we find them?"

Sam reached into his pocket and pulled out a paper. "Got their numbers. We'll find them. I sent them ahead. I wanted them on a bus. I wanted to make sure they were headed to safety. They're with Reverend Ray and…and Bill."

"Bill? Our neighbor?"

"Yep, he said he wasn't sick. He was right."

"That's good. Real good. How did you end up here?" I asked.

"I wanted to wait. I wanted to wait until the very last minute to go. Just in case, you know, you showed up and someone would be here to tell you what was going on. I kept hoping you'd be here. Gotta tell you…this…" He kissed Tag. "Is a surprise. A great one."

"We woke up yesterday and the fever broke."

"So it wasn't the flu?"

I shrugged. "I don't know. I do know I would not be on this bus if it wasn't for Luis." I reached up and tapped Luis on the shoulder. "Luis?"

He turned around.

"Sam, meet my friend Luis."

Luis extended his hand back to Sam. "Pleasure."

"Thank you for getting our girl and boy here," Sam said. "Are you alone?"

Before he could answer, I did. "No Sam, he's with us now. Is that okay, Luis? You'll travel with us and our family."

"I would like that."

"So would we." I exhaled. Luis turned back around, slid into his seat. I could see he was finally relieved after the insane attempt to get to the transport. He rested his head against the window.

With Tag on Sam's lap, I too relaxed and tilted my head to his shoulder. I was so damn grateful and moved beyond belief that Sam hadn't given up on us. He had a lot of information to share, things he learned while waiting on me. We had a long trip ahead and a lot of time for me to listen.

FORTY-ONE - RETAINED

Chaos, confusion and misinterpretation were the things Sam said he heard about. While waiting for me and the last transport, he spoke to anyone that would talk to him. He found out that the country was thrown into a plethora of emotions and for the first couple days things went out of control. They tried to instill law and order and after several days they had a plan.

"We heard the west coast was gone," a soldier told us. "It wasn't until people started coming east, that everyone realized it wasn't wiped out."

"So they knew what happened?" I asked.

"Pretty much, we knew right away. The EMP from it wiped out most of the electronics. Only those who saw it coming were ready. They got a message out to FEMA. It was a domino effect. Once one place got power, others did. Not a lot but enough to keep getting the word out."

His word, he claimed, was not gospel. Most of what he got was third or fourth hand information. When it hit he was working his day job at a gas station. At the realization that it was something big, he hurried to the reserve base. It took two days after that for him to be officially activated. The soldier was from Missouri.

Initially it was believed the cloud of smoke would move with the fire. But as of recently, information Sam hadn't received, the cloud had moved north to north east.

It moved north of Los Angeles into Nevada, from Denver to Minnesota. Rendering everything above that line a dead zone, covered by a thick smoke that blocked out any light.

Once the fire reached its furthest distance, the hole in the ozone layer would keep it simmering. Until the cloud cleared, the north would be thrust into an ice age, and eventually that cloud, though thinner would encircle the globe, causing everyone to live in a gray colder world for at least two years.

A world still survivable with preparation. Unfortunately, people out east, were holding on to what they had, not giving into survival migration and hoping for the best.

Sam said he heard there were 'gray' areas. "No pun intended to the clouds," he said. "Places that experts don't know if they will be effected. Meaning western parts of some states like Pennsylvania."

Dark and cloud were the least of the worries, the easiest battle. The new flu was a killer in more ways than one. It was a variation of the bird flu. When the birds and the people migrated, they pushed the flu into new territories. There were also multiple cases of Hantavirus as well from the migration of rodents from the heat.

The disease spread faster than the fire and smoke. Bringing illness and death as far as the refugees went. No one knew if the flu started because of the event or if the event just expedited something that had already begun.

Did it matter?

There were no resources put into fighting the flu. Just treating those who were sick. The majority of effort had to be placed on a long term survival plan and finding locations for millions who had relocated.

Of course, that was the word from those in the middle of the country. Most had not even been east. There were rumors, because the east was only decimated by illness and lack of power, that they were still battling chaos and violence.

"We are moved in phases," Sam said. "Your travel stopping points will depend on where your displacement camp is located. From what I heard they been expediting camps for four days. Not a lot of time."

"So we don't know where this transport is going?" I asked.

Someone from the bus heard my question and answered, "Heard because we're small we're going to New Brunswick. That's where a lot of the volunteers are going after they wrap up their stations."

The volunteers were moving in waves across the country as we were. The Arena was originally a medical holding place while waiting on transport. Anyone too ill to travel would wait for the next transport. The medical people and their resources had moved out a day earlier.

I was confused and hated the fact that I wouldn't have any concrete information until I arrived wherever I was going. I didn't really know what was happening to the north, no one really did.

Our first leg in the trip came to an end late afternoon at Holloman Air Force Base, New Mexico. It was one of seven transport stops in the area, but the only one remaining open. The stopping station had electricity, it was wonderful, and running water. I asked if I could bathe, and was told it was a good idea.

Did I smell?

We'd stay there for the rest of the day and leave at the very earliest the next morning. It all depended on if there were still a lot of ill at the next stopping point.

"They don't want to run the healthy into the sick," a doctor told me. "Once that wave of people moves out, we can move in there."

A doctor.

He was young, almost too young for my liking. I didn't ask his credentials and didn't know if he were military or a local doctor. I was escorted to him, along with Tag because we were pale and looked ill.

More so me, I was told. That surprised me considering Tag was the one who'd been at death's door.

Immediately when we arrived we were given blood tests. Not everyone, just a select few. Then after a couple hours we were brought in to be examined by the young doctor, named Jesse.

Tag was checked out first. I told the doctor that I believed he didn't have the flu, because he survived. I was corrected. The blood tests showed he had immunities, meaning he had the virus.

"He's made it thought he worst of it. There were low levels of radiation exposure. Very low, under one hundred rad," he said. "He may experience some symptoms considering his low immunities. But nothing he won't handle. That's one tough boy."

"Yes, he is."

"You on the other hand…"

Me? I knew I was not feeling well. I told the girls I was sick. I truly believed that had to do more so with my emotional state.

Until I was examined.

It was my first post delivery check up since I lost the baby four days earlier.

Jesse expressed how he was sorry to hear about my loss, then ran down his laundry list.

"You were exposed to radiation as well. The other fellow, too. Luis? Nothing we can't treat. Probably because the three of you were in the hot zone. Your platelets are down. Loss of blood will do that. That's one of the reasons you are so pale."

"I stopped bleeding." I said. "What's the other reason?"

"When I examined you, something didn't feel right. The loss of the baby was abrupt. The placenta detached, probably a day or so before the loss. And you have what we call a retained placenta. Meaning part of it is still in the uterus. It started an infection. We need to do an extraction then get you on antibiotics. Another day and you would have died."

I knew I wasn't well, but that ill? I was surprised to hear it. Jesse explained that if I wasn't better by the time the transport was ready to leave, I'd have to wait until the facility packed up and left.

Another delay.

I didn't want to wait any longer. I wanted Tag to be reunited with Nicole. She was carrying the grief of losing her child and needed to know he was alright.

We needed to lift that from her.

I realized I needed to get better and Tag need to stop, rest and heal as well. I just hoped the delay didn't complicate finding Nicole and Julie.

Getting east to survive wasn't my goal. My goal was to get my entire family back together to take on survival as a whole.

FORTY-TWO - WAITING GAME

Fort Ticonderoga, NY
September 24 – Two months later

Our departure was not only delayed due to my health, but we were stuck waiting until the stopping point was packed up and ready to go as well. It was four days before we left, and following that was another three day delay in Hays, Kansas.

That delay wasn't due to illness, but rather civil unrest that developed in the east.

The flames had held tight, devouring what was left of the land out west. There was no longer a blue sky, and the days of sweating were long gone.

Temperatures had dropped to an average of fifty.

Farmers across the country were scurrying to save what they could of supplies, while countless others worked on a plan to grow food in the cold.

Traveling with the Holloman crew had its perks. There were a lot of important military personnel, along with doctors. I believed we were surrounded by valuable resources that could help me find my children. Especially since they kept on telling us they'd help once we got settled.

Our eastern end destination was no longer New Brunswick, but the historical Fort Ticonderoga, NY. When we arrived the on the first of August, I wondered if another type of apocalypse was about to occur. The wide old walls of the main complex looked like some sort of fort for against a zombie outbreak.

I was assured it wasn't and it was now the main government hub because it was easy to secure the officials from the unrest, and far enough away.

We were in a camp three miles away from the fort. Fortunately, we were able to ride down to the New Haven site. I was hopeful, until we arrived. Tens of thousands of white trailers packed the small area.

We gave the girls' numbers to the main desk.

They were never there.

Check.

Check again.

They never arrived. It was possible, someone told me that, like us, they got delayed and ended up going somewhere else.

Our best hope was to stay close to Fort Ticonderoga, because eventually all information would flow there.

We were issued a small trailer for me, Sam, Luis and Tag. Every day I walked to the main complex, hoping and asking if someone could help me find my daughters. It was useless because there were no computers with a major database. Just paperwork that didn't always make its way to us.

Finally, Luis took a job as a food truck driver. It was one of the most dangerous jobs there was. But he claimed he was bored and it was a risk worth taking because he would cover the most area and could look for the girls.

By mid August, the snow started to fall. Luis would return every four days. Rest a day then go back out again. Each time we'd hear the truck, we'd race to the window to look.

Did he find them? Was he alone?

Each time he returned he was hopeful. "Not yet, but next trip is to Boston."

Or whatever place he was scheduled to go.

We were secluded up in that area, but the population wasn't restricted to the camps. Those who lived in the east stayed in their homes and many left the camps for a better place. I couldn't see the girls leaving a registered place. Not when they knew Sam was out there.

We celebrated Labor Day with a massive snowstorm that officially marked the start to the nuclear winter.

The next day was the last day I saw Luis. He went for a run and didn't return.

Still, snow piled high, I walked to the complex, every day. They knew me by name.

No word about my girls. No word about Luis.

As time rolled by, not only did the weather become worse, but with each desolate looking day that passed, I lost hope.

FORTY-THREE - SARDINES

November 8

We were fortunate. We had lucked into a privileged area. Government, military and important people lived in and around Fort Ticonderoga. I was told our food rations were outstanding compared to other places.

That surprised me. I was always hungry. At the beginning of the month we were given one case of MRE's and weekly we would pick up rations. Rations that included minimal water, fresh flat bread, beans and some sort meat. Whether it was canned or fresh.

We held high hopes for fresh vegetables that were being grown in the greenhouse and hydro farms.

Having much more than anyone else placed us in a high security area. Although the bad weather kept the marauders away.

Sam had taken a job at the complex as a radio monitor, and I took a job separating rations. A job that not only got me an extra can or two as pay, but kept me in the loop of looking for my family.

The three of us, Sam, me and Tag walked to the complex. Every morning it was the same thing.

"Morning, Donna," I'd say. "Any connections made?"

"Sorry, Tess. Not yet."

Then the evening would come with me asking Sam the same questions. Only to get the same answer.

Nothing.

Twenty-seven million people had moved. Some registered some not.

Finding them was going to be nearly impossible.

I was working my job, sitting at my desk behind the little window. Men and women who ran the trucks from one stock to another would drop off supplies at that window. No one was allowed to come into that room. I would register them and shelve them accordingly.

If it were an item grabbed from stockpile, they'd state it and I'd call out what they turned in.

If they grabbed it from a home or abandoned shop, they were marked as such and handed out immediately because their freshness was unknown.

A woman named Susan was an ace at finding stuff. She would clutter my counter with items every time she arrived.

"Dead prepper," she said and placed a box on the counter. "There are six more."

"Are you shitting me?" I asked.

"No. Came across the house. Owner was dead, had tons of dried stuff in the basement. Gold mine."

"Good job."

Susan proudly handed each box to me. I counted the items out loud, wrote them down, when I finished she signed the sheet. It was close to Thanksgiving, some of the dried goods would be a treat.

"Hey," she said and slipped her gloved hand forward. "For Tag." She lifted her hand and exposed a bag of M and M's.

"Susan…"

"Shh. Candy doesn't have to be registered." She winked. "Tell him it's from Aunt Sue."

"I will. Thank you."

She left. I placed the candy in my sweater pocket, grabbed the last box and took it to the shelf. I wasn't paying attention when I returned. I had sat down, pulled the paperwork forward, when a can of sardines, a single can, was set on the desk.

"What did you do? Feel guilty about keeping it?" I asked with a laugh.

"No, you gave it to me," a male voice said. "I did not eat it and thought you'd want it back since you collect rations."

Slowly I lifted my eyes.

I screamed his name as I jumped to my feet. "Luis!" I flung open the door and raced out, blasting him with my body and arms. "I thought you were dead."

"I you sent many messages, but none made it through, I suppose. I was stuck in Virginia. They wouldn't let me return. I had a government truck, so I had to stay there." He pulled back some and placed his hands on my shoulders. "I never stopped looking for your girls. I carried their numbers." He patted his chest pocket.

"I know. Thank you."

"I never stopped…" he said. "Until I found them."

Was he joking? I locked eyes with him and his eyes squinted with a smile.

I felt everything inside of me tremble and when he sidestepped his tall body, I saw my girls.

Julie carried Liam on her hip, he had grown so much. The girls looked healthy and fine. A little thin, but weren't we all.

I cried out so loudly, I was afraid security was going to come.

The Mommys and Marmies along with tears were in abundance as we embraced and cried.

Then it hit me.

"Did he tell you?" I asked Nicole

"Tell me what?"

I looked at Luis.

"No. I want you to do so." Luis said.

"Tell us what?" asked Julie. "He said nothing about you being alive either. Only that Sam was looking for us."

"I wanted it to be a surprise," said Luis. "It needed to be a surprise."

"Where...where's Josh?" I asked.

Nicole lowered her head. "He died of the flu right after we left. That's why we didn't end up in New Haven. We had to wait for another transport. They didn't register us there. But he was sick. Real sick like Tag."

It was so sad that we had lost Josh, I needed moment to absorb that, to grieve that, but my insides were jumping with excitement over seeing my children and telling Nicole.

But instead of telling her, I grabbed her hand and started to run.

"Where are we going?" she asked.

"Mom, wait, I can't run with Liam." Julie called out. "Why are we running?"

I didn't answer, I just flew down the hall to the small room where the children had school. There were seven of them in there.

Without knocking, I opened the door. "Sorry Miss Beasley." I apologized. "Can I see...?"

"Tag!" Nicole screamed. "Oh my God."

The second Tag cried out, "Mommy!" Nicole couldn't walk. She tried but her legs gave way and she dropped to the floor as Tag charged to her and leapt into her long awaited arms.

There's a sound in the cry a mother makes when she loses her child. A sound only a mother could make. I never knew the opposite could occur when a mother was reunited with a child she believed was lost.

"I thought you were gone." Nicole sobbed. Her hands feeling and grasping Tag. "I thought you both were gone."

Julie raced toward the room and I stopped her for a moment to kiss her, then released her to hold Tag.

Reaching out, I grabbed onto Luis. There were no words. I couldn't thank him enough.

Wrapping my arms around his waist, I saw Sam at the end of the corridor.

"Tell me it's true," he said breathily. "Tell me."

I nodded.

Sam's hip had been giving him trouble since the weather turned bitterly cold, but he moved faster than I had seen him move in months.

Another interruption, a good interruption into Miss Beasley's class.

I looked up at Luis. He smiled from ear to ear. Did he know the magnitude of what he did? What he meant to us? I hoped he did. This big man with a huge heart, rolled into our lives and became the angel we needed in a dire situation.

From the hall I watched as they all embraced. The other kids asking Tag if that was his mom. Laughter, tears and hugs. It was phenomenal. I could also tell that Liam was different and Julie, not Nicole, had taken that mother role. She just was so mature with him.

"Don't you want to go and join?" Luis asked.

"No, I am enjoying watching."

I could stand there forever and watch. It saddened me to think Josh, with all that he had done, didn't make it. Did his family know? Were they, like me, searching desperately for their son? If they didn't know, that would be my next goal. No parent should go through life not knowing what happened to their child. No matter the outcome, it had to be known, resolved.

The reunion continued and I supposed it would for a long time. We were separated for months. Never knowing about the other. Left with only guessing and hoping.

All that was behind us.

It didn't matter what became of the world. It didn't matter if it were cold and gray, dying and desperate. It seemed a lot less dismal and lot more doable in the wake of having my family back.

We had our losses, great losses. This was a victory. A long awaited victory. We were reunited. That was all that mattered.

There was a long road of hardship behind us and an even longer road ahead. It was a journey to into an uncertain future, one that we would take as a family unit.

Apart, yes, we would survive. But together we do more than just survive…we live.

Thank you so much for reading this book. I hope you enjoyed it. Please visit my website www.jacquelinedruga.com and sign up for my mailing list for updates and new releases.

Your support is invaluable to me. I welcome and respond to your feedback. Please feel free to email me at greatoneas@gmail.com

Made in the USA
Monee, IL
03 January 2020